THE COST *of* BETRAYAL

PART I

W.C. HOLLOWAY

"AMERICA'S NEW STORY TELLER"

GOOD 2 GO PUBLISHING

COST OF BETRAYAL: PART I
Written by W.C. Holloway
Cover Design: Davida Baldwin – Odd Ball Designs
Typesetter: Mychea
ISBN: 978-1-947340-46-6
Copyright © 2019 Good2Go Publishing
Published 2019 by Good2Go Publishing
7311 W. Glass Lane • Laveen, AZ 85339
www.good2gopublishing.com
https://twitter.com/good2gobooks
G2G@good2gopublishing.com
www.facebook.com/good2gopublishing
www.instagram.com/good2gopublishing

PROLOGUE

Betrayal, the word alone stings deep as you reflect back to the one(s) that caused you so much pain, or even caused you financial strain. Betrayal comes from greed and always thinking what you have is not enough—be that physical, emotional, or financial. Betrayal is the fear of losing it all or being taken away from something or someone, so you turn your back on it all. You save yourself from suffering at the cost of many being incarcerated due to your betrayal. Betrayal is a bitch that is worse than karma, yet worthy of a bullet to bring it all to an end

CHAPTER 1

Spanish Harlem is known as a place for getting money from every angle and aspect. Young Pablo, one of Spanish Harlem's own, was nicknamed after Pablo Escobar. Just like Escobar, Young Pablo was serious about his money and would lay down anyone who fucked with his money or anyone on his team that didn't show him loyalty. He was also known in the underground drug world as the youngest kingpin. At twenty-one years old, he was in charge with plenty of product. He stood five foot ten and weighed close to two hundred pounds. He got his medium build from hitting the weights when he could. His thick eyebrows and black-colored eyes only added to his dark stare when necessary. Being so young and in power, and having that much money and product so fast, he did not trust anyone other than those closest to him, because they all grew up together since they were only knee-high. He wore his haircut close just like his mustache, while the rest of his face was clean-shaven to show off his youthful side.

Today, Young Pablo was in the back of the bodega he owned and was accompanied by his team. They were counting money and running thousands of dollars at a time through the digital counters. There was not too much talking going on, since it was all about getting down to the final count of the money made. The only sound other than cell phones chiming was the digital counter flipping through the money.

His team sat back as he grabbed the money from the machines, took the count, and added up the totals from each of his homeboys. The money was short, which was certainly not a good look for whoever shorted it.

"Hey, Gordo, you picked up this money before you came over here, right?" Young Pablo asked.

"Yeah, why?"

"My money is short again. That's what's wrong! Now you're either taking yours off the top and thinking that them motherfuckers is giving you all of the money, or somebody is fucking with my shit."

Hearing Young Pablo raise his voice made the other members of the crew clench their weapons, even though Gordo had been on the team since day one. But they were always ready to ride with and for Young Pablo.

Gordo wiped the sweat from his forehead and had flashbacks of the people he had helped Young Pablo kill for fucking with his money or coming up short. But now he was in the same position having to explain himself.

"Wait a minute, bro. I fucking gave the money to Flaco like I always do. Pablo, you know I don't fuck around when it comes to this paper, bro. I got like $900. This is my walk-around bread," Gordo said, speaking fast to make his point.

Young Pablo stared down his homie and saw that he was speaking the truth.

"Everybody have a seat and put their guns away!" Young Pablo ordered, before focusing his attention to Flaco. "So you grabbed the bag from him, right?" he asked Flaco.

Flaco was a thugged-out Puerto Rican raised in Harlem. He linked up with Young Pablo four years ago, unlike the rest of the crew. Things always ran smoothly until now. The loco Latino stood six foot even. His beard was closely shaped up and flowed with his braids and tweezed eyebrows. He went about his business in the streets and had taken out people for young Pablo. Flaco never had a problem being skinny because he would put big niggas and big-mouth muthafuckas in their place.

Young Pablo leaned back in his seat while still clenching the stack of money as he nodded his head to his squad. They already knew what he was hitting for, so they jumped up and all pulled out their weapons. At the same time, Flaco reacted just as quickly and grabbed his Glock 9 mm.

"I let you in my circle, and you think you can just help yourself to mi money?" Young Pablo snapped.

"I don't know what the fuck you thinking, like I'ma steal from you, but I'm not going out like that!" Flaco called out while pointing his guy at Young Pablo and pissing him off even more.

"Fifty stacks is missing, asshole, and it didn't just walk away, and you're the last one to touch the bag before it got to me," Young Pablo said while still leaning in the chair with his hand on his gun at his waist line. "You've been taking a lot of trips to Vegas. What, you fucking ya money up, so you steal mine?" he asked, looking at his team and wanting them to kill the muthafucking traitor.

"You want these muthafuckas to shoot me? They shoot me, I shoot you!" he snapped.

Young Pablo remained calm and leaned back in his chair. He knew his team could handle this.

"Don't worry, Flaco, you're dead to me now. You'll never make it out of here alive. Even if you do, I know where your whole family lives, including that pretty bitch you got the kids with. Kill him!" he shouted.

Flaco did not hesitate to pull the trigger on Young Pablo as he fired off shots that slammed into his body and thrust him out of the chair. At the same time, he took off running toward the back door exit. Gordo and the rest of the crew fired on him as he ran away.

Flaco was hit from the slugs, yet in fear of dying, he opened the door and took off running down the alleyway as the gang followed right behind him. They fired off more slugs and dropped Flaco at the end of the alleyway. Upon seeing him drop, they wanted to go finish him off when they heard sirens.

"Fuck that piece of shit! Leave him to die. We have to go get Young Pablo and take him to the hospital!"

"Young Pablo's going to be okay, bro. We shot that punta!" Gordo said while helping him up as his boys grabbed his legs and rushed him out to the car to take him to the hospital.

Young Pablo was in the back seat opening and closing his eyes while going in and out of consciousness. He was trying to hold on after being struck in the chest by the slugs. However, the shots punctured his lung, which made it hard for him to breathe. Gordo drove fast while at the same time snapping about what just had taken place.

"This is some fucked-up shit, bro! You alright back there?"

"He's good, bro! Just drive!" Pito ordered while holding him in his arms. "You're going to make it, Pablo. We gotta still get this money out here," Pito added, trying to make his homie feel better while also trying to keep him alert.

Pito was the youngster of the crew at only eighteen, but he was very streetwise for his age. The five-foot-ten, 175-pound Puerto Rican wore his haircut close and faded on the sides. He was a real pretty boy with a baby face, but he loved this thugging shit and always got a thrill out of busting his guns.

Within minutes of running a few red lights, they made it to the hospital and pulled up to the emergency room entrance. They rushed Young Pablo through the doors and called out to the nurses.

"Help me! My homie got shot. He's bleeding bad!" Gordo yelled out, fearing the worst for Young Pablo after seeing him spit out blood.

"What's your friend's name?" the nurse asked as she rushed over to help him.

"Enrico Alverez," Gordo replied as they rushed Young Pablo through the ER doors.

He did not leave; instead, he paced back and forth

hoping his homie would make it.

Pito, Chico, and Kilo raced back to the bodega with hopes of tracking down Flaco and finishing him off. They also needed to secure the money.

Gordo remained in the waiting room and called up Young Pablo's older sister, Catrina, "Kitty Cat" Alverez. She was two years older than him yet a powerful boss in the heroin game. She was known as La Primera Dama de Calles: the First Lady of the Streets. At first glance, the five-foot-five Latina could easily be a magazine cover girl or video vixen with her long, silky black hair and grayish-colored eyes that always seemed to sparkle under the light. Dimples in her smile only added to her allure, but she was a rare beauty that was deadly if you crossed her. She had the body of a goddess, perfectly measured in all the right places, with perky breasts and a nice ass that always looked good in the latest fashions.

Cat was at home in her $2 million, six thousand-square-foot Manhattan high-rise with floor-to-ceiling views when her cell phone sounded off the call from Gordo.

"Hey, how are you, Gordo?"

"Not good, Cat. Your brother got shot. I'm at the hospital with him now."

Upon hearing that her baby brother had been shot, a wave of anger ran throughout her body. She instantly wanted to get revenge on whoever shot him as well as anyone in her way of getting to this person.

"Who did this?" she asked while clenching the cell phone to her ear.

"That bastard Flaco. Pablo caught him stealing."

"Where the fuck was everybody when this took place?" she snapped, wanting to blame someone.

"Cat, Cat! We shot that muthafucka, but he still ran down the back alleyway of the bodega. We bounced when we heard the sirens, plus we had to get Pablo to the hospital."

"I'm on my way. Don't let anything else happen to my brother," she ordered before hanging up.

Gordo knew Cat was going to unleash her wrath on Flaco and maybe even the team if she deemed that they had dropped the ball protecting her brother.

CHAPTER 2

Meanwhile back at the bodega, Pito, Chico, and Kilo drove by and saw the cops marking with orange cones where the shells that were fired had landed. At the same, they secured the area with yellow tape. They then looked down the alleyway. No Flaco. His car was still sitting on the corner, which meant someone had come to get him. The trio could not get to the money now, so they would have to come back later when everything had died down.

"I knew I should have killed that piece of shit before we left," Pito said, after not seeing the man's body lying at the end of the alleyway.

"He didn't go to the hospital, because we just left there. This means he had somebody else come get him," Chico added.

"Let's go to his baby momma's crib. I bet that bitch came by and picked him up," Kilo suggested.

Pito drove over that way, which took about ten minutes to get to. When they arrived, he drove slowly as they all scanned the area to make sure Flaco did not have any lookouts. Nothing. Not too many people were out and about.

"Pito, pull over here and we'll all walk over to her crib. I see her truck parked in front of her crib, so he might be up in there," Kilo said.

They made their way up to the crib with their guns out ready to take care of business. At the same time Pito was ready to knock on the door, Alexi, Flaco's baby momma, came to the door looking like she was ready to leave in a hurry.

"Where are you going, Alexi?" Pito asked.

Alexi was Flaco's ride-or-die baby momma and

on-and-off again girlfriend. She was sexy but deceiving with short hair, brown eyes, a pretty smile, a thick ass and thighs, little breasts but a mouth full, and a flat stomach. She did not look like she had two kids with Flaco.

"I, I'm going to my mom's to get my kids," she responded, clearly startled by their presence.

"She's lying, bro. This bitch is probably getting ready to go meet that piece of shit!" Chico said.

Pito took out his Glock 17 mm and placed it against her flat stomach. He had the same thoughts as Chico.

"Where is he, Alexi? If you lie, I'll leave you right here in this doorway!" Pito warned, ready to put in work.

"What's wrong with you? I thought he was your homeboy?" she questioned in fear.

"He fucked up, and I think you know this by now, because you probably were going to meet him before you ran into us," Kilo said. "Now tell us where he is and where the fuck was you about to go?"

She froze in place while processing what was going on and what they were asking of her. She could not give up the man she loved and who was the father of her two children.

"She's stalling, bro. We got to find this mutha-fucka!" Chico said.

Pito wanted answers, so he reacted fast. He took his gun and slapped her across the face hard, stinging her flesh and inflicting pain as she dropped into the doorway.

"You fag! Flaco is going to kill all you puntas for touching me! You know he don't play that shit!"

"You dumb-ass bitch! All you have to do is let us

know where he is!" Pito said with aggression.

As she lay there holding her face, her cell phone sounded off and played a love song by Royce, which let the crew know it was Flaco calling. At the same time they figured this out, she hurried to answer her phone.

"Flaco, help me! Help me, Pito—!"

"Give me the phone, you stupid bitch!" Pito screamed, jamming his gun into her stomach before snatching the phone. He put the phone to his ear. "You fucked up, Flaco! We got ya baby momma, and we know where everybody else lives, too!"

"Pito, if you touch her, I'll bury all of you motherfuckers! You hear me!"

"No, asshole, do you hear me!" Pito snapped back, firing a round into Alexi's stomach and inflicting intense pain on her as the hot slug burned her flesh.

"Aaaaggh! Fagot! Flaco, he shot me!" Alexi cried in pain.

"Pito, I promise on my life that no one is safe. I'll come for all of y'all!"

Flaco hung up the phone. He knew he could not save Alexi from the crew, because he was hurt, in a bad position, and too far away from her.

"Last chance, punta! Now tell me where he is?" Pito ordered while still pointing his gun at her.

Alexi remained strong but in pain, and she allowed her anger to get the best of her by revealing where he was.

"He's with the Black Mafia. They're going to wipe all of y'all out one by one, motherfuckers! So fuck you, Pito!"

"As pretty as you are, Alexi, I wouldn't mind.

But that's personal and this is business," Pito said before firing off a slug into her face and marring her beauty forever.

Her head twisted from the impact of the bullet and she was killed instantly. Her body slumped in the doorway as they all took off running, jumping into the car, and then racing off back to the hospital.

The car ride back to the hospital was quiet for each of the young men as they thought about Alexi's last words about Flaco being with the Black Mafia. It was an organization that was powerful and strong in the city, and also known to be associated with one of the nation's most powerful Italian Mafia crime families.

"The Black Mafia is who his bitch ass ran to, huh?" Kilo said.

"That asshole must have been fucking with them

behind our backs for them to just come at him like that, bro," Chico suggested.

"Fuck them motherfuckers, bro. They bleed just like us!" Pito said, hyped up and waving his gun around. "I'll put a bullet in their face just like I'ma do to Flaco's bitch ass!"

"Yo, bro, stop waving that gun around like that. You see I'm driving, and that shit could go off or something," Chico begged.

"My bad, bro. This shit got me pissed right now."

"After we leave the hospital, I'll put word out in the streets to track him down," Kilo spoke up.

Chico was five foot ten with a medium build. He had a bald head and was clean-shaven. His dark stare and thick eyebrows only added to his murderous look, as did the teardrop tattoos spelling out the words Body Count. Chico was a ride-or-die goon about his money and street credibility. Respect was everything to him, and Flaco disrespected the entire crew with his betrayal.

Kilo stood six foot even and had long black hair pulled back to expose his well-groomed pretty-boy features of tweezed eyebrows and a close-cut beard shaped up with razor perfection. He too loved the getting-money shit along with getting all of the ladies that appreciated him. At the same time, he would lay down anyone that disrespected him or his team. Like most Latinos in this game, he went by the code of the streets: Drugs, money, and blood. Flaco now had to pay in blood for betraying that code.

CHAPTER 3

An hour had passed by and Young Pablo was out of surgery and back in his room. He was resting with his team present, along with his sister, Kitty Cat, who came with her girls, Princess and Mya. Cat sat at his bedside caressing his face with sisterly love, as his eyes were closed peacefully sleeping off the medication.

"Bro, I'm going to get these fools that did this to you," Cat promised, wanting Flaco's blood for his betrayal.

Princess, one of Cat's homegirls, was Puerto Rican-born and about her business, yet she had seen a lot in the ghettos of San Juan. This made her vicious when necessary; however, no one would be able to tell at first glance upon seeing her beauty. She stood five foot two and was thick in all the right places. She weighed 130 perfectly placed pounds and had long silky black hair that flowed over her 36 Cs. Her luring smile with diamond dimple piercings added to her look, along with her glowing green-hazel eyes.

Cat's other ride-or-die bitch, Mya, was beautiful but just as deceptive with hazel-brown eyes and light brown hair with golden blonde highlights that added to her sex appeal. She stood five foot seven and weighed 140. She had a flat stomach with an ass to follow. She, too, was all about getting the money and making people pay for wronging her or her crew.

"Look, Pito! I want the streets to know that I want Flaco brought in alive so he can pay for his betrayal and bloodshed against my family," Catrina addressed him and the crew.

"His baby momma said he's with them Black

Mafia muthafuckas," Kilo interjected.

"Then I'll get word to them through the people I know. The end result is his blood on my hands!" Cat said, wanting to kill him personally while looking into his eyes as he took his last breath.

"I'm ready to dead all of them muthafuckas, including them Black Mafia niggas for protecting him!" Pito said, all hyped up as always.

"Flaco's mine, Pito, so don't lose sight of that. I know he hurt your homeboy, but he is my brother, so I'll deal with him personally. If the Black Mafia doesn't see to my terms once I reach out to them, then they'll see the wrath I bring!" Catrina warned.

While they continued figuring out what their game plan would be to reach out to the Black Mafia and track down Flaco, Young Pablo started to come around upon hearing voices in the room. He then opened his eyes and saw everyone standing around.

"Did y'all get that muthafucka?" he questioned.

They all instantly shifted their attention to him. They were happy he was awake, especially his sister, who looked on at him with sisterly love while still caressing his face.

"Hey, brother. I'm glad to see you with your eyes open. Everything is going to be okay. I'll take care of this, don't worry. Your team shot him, but he got away."

"How did he get away?"

"Them Black Mafia niggas, bro. He must be in with them or something," Chico said.

Young Pablo did not like the sound of this, knowing how the Black Mafia was affiliated with the Italian Mafia. He needed to be at 100 percent in order to deal with this problem and move all the way out and conduct business as usual.

"Sister, I don't want war. I only want Flaco, understand?"

"Baby bro, he's with them not by accident but by choice, which leads me to believe they dealt with him for financial means. So getting him back is going to cost money or blood."

"She's right, papi. They're not going to protect Flaco unless they have a financial interest to protect," Princess added.

"Whatever choice is made, we are all here for you and your sister," Mya said, all ready to take care of business.

"Yeah, bro, we got you, plus we got Cat and her sexy-ass girls that will catch all of them Black Mafia muthafuckas off guard!" Pito explained.

Young Pablo lay his head back down, closed his

eyes, and became silent as he processed his thoughts on the situation that was unfolding with or without him. Flaco's slimy and greedy ass had started it all. He wished he would have just put a bullet into his head without even asking about the money. Now he and whoever was protecting him would have to pay at any cost.

Everyone in the room noticed that the young boss had become quiet, so they all excused themselves from the room except for Gordo. He stayed behind to look after his homeboy until he got better.

Unlike most people his age, when Young Pablo started in the game, he did not buy new clothes, jewelry, sneakers, or cars. He stacked his bread on every flip, which allowed him to keep rising until he met his Cuban connect in Little Havana, Florida. With him now being in his high position, he knew that when the streets heard about him being hit up in the hospital, they would try to take over his blocks, but neither he nor his team would have this. No one was going to come between him and his empire.

CHAPTER 4

On the other side of the city, Flaco found himself laid up in a warehouse owned and operated by the Black Mafia. He lay on a table as the contracted doctor worked on pulling the bullets from his flesh, followed by stitching him up and placing bandages on him.

"Aggh, Doc, that shit hurts!" Flaco cried out, feeling the bullet being pulled from his thigh, which was one of four places he was hit, along with his back, side, and shoulder. These were wounds that could easily have become fatal if not tended to.

"Stop your fucking crying! This doctor is the best in the game. Besides, without him, you die!" Blanco stated.

Blanco was the number-two guy in the Black

Mafia organization, the underboss and enforcer. The Harlem-born bi-racial goon was half-Puerto Rican and half-Black, which gave him the best of both worlds and allowed him to speak English and Spanish. He stood six foot three and had a medium build. He was business savvy, and he knew his way around the streets and the legal business in which he helped move money around. He wore a close-cut flow with his close beard shaped up weekly by his barber. He was well dressed, groomed, and manicured at all times, and he looked the role of an underboss of the most lucrative black organization in the nation, next to the New York Bloods, who really knew how to make money.

Blanco allowed Flaco to hustle in his hood and different parts of the city where the Black Mafia had an interest; however, it came at a cost of 20 percent of all monies made or a flat weekly fee. Blanco knew Young Pablo's team had the best product in the city, so he felt why not benefit from it. The only downside for Flaco was that he had gotten carried away with spending and living outside his means, and it finally caught up to him.

As the doctor was finishing up bandaging Flaco's wounds, Blanco began to address the financial factor in this matter.

"My man Flaco, good medical attention comes with a cost, as you may know. Our family doctor comes where he's needed and at any time, and this in itself isn't cheap," he said, looking on at Flaco now sitting up and facing him with a look of confusion, as if he did not understand what was being said.

"What are you talking about, bro?"

"My words are clear. You needed my doctor, and

without question you'll also need my family's assistance since you betrayed your team, who we all know won't let this pass by."

Blanco was in the company of a few soldiers as well as his known go-to guy and street enforcer, Tek-9, a twenty-two-year-old goon that stood five foot nine and was a solid two hundred pounds from working out up state for two years until his release last year. Tek-9's dark skin and dark stare taunted those in his presence, because no one knew if their turn was coming when he was around. Besides, Tek-9 was always on that wet, which made him look even crazier and ready to put work in.

Flaco focused on Blanco, since he did want to look at Tek-9 just in case he caught a complex about something he thought he had seen.

"I got a hundred stacks at the crib. I can get that

to you now or whenever you want it," Flaco said.

"That'll be a start for now."

"Whoa, bro! What do you mean for now? That's all the bread I have, other than these few stacks in my pocket."

"That $100,000 is the doctor's fee. Now we have to talk about the cost of protecting you from them crazy-ass homeboys you run with, because they're not going to lay down—and war costs money."

Flaco did not have any more money other than what he had on him. He did not want the Black Mafia to turn its back on him, so his mind started racing while trying to figure out what he was going to do to prevail being murdered by Young Pablo and those he would surely send for him, because they loved him in Spanish Harlem.

"I got something even better. I can give you the

location to Young Pablo's stash house with the product. There's enough to finance my protection and more, where you can give me a few bricks when your team is done."

Blanco appreciated the sound of money he could gather from the stash house take, which could generate hundreds of thousands of dollars for him and the family. Like most men, he was motivated by money and the power it provided.

Blanco did not respond right away, because he did not want to seem pressed. He then glanced over at Tek-9, who was looking serious, high as a muthafucka, and ready to bust out his gun.

"Okay, my friend, give me the address," Blanco requested.

Flaco was so much of a scumbag and always willing to stay ahead and save himself that he gave up Young Pablo's stash house. With this new information, Blanco was going to send his men to take out the stash house and secure the product and money if any was found.

"The spot is in my old hood. Nobody goes to that crib unless it's for business. It's his aunt's crib, so it'll just be her and three other people all strapped, so don't slip. The product could be anywhere in the crib since he always puts it in different places each time, but check the bedroom, living room, and kitchen, or just make that bitch tell you where it is."

"Flaco, I'ma send my man Tek-9 over there with a few other Black Mafia soldiers to secure this tomorrow. It better be official, or Tek-9 will be back to pay you a visit," Blanco threatened, as he walked toward the exit of the warehouse.

Flaco yelled out as Blanco walked away. He

wanted him to know that he was not lying, because he did not want Tek-9 to come at him.

"Yo, Blanco, I'm keeping it real, bro. There should be at least fifty to sixty kilos left because he had three hundred but we moved a lot of it, and the rest he has around the city."

"If this is true, your life insurance is good and you'll have the family's protection," Blanco promised him, while still walking through the door and out to his charcoal-gray 5600 Mercedes Benz.

He slipped on his new white-and-gold Sean Jean aviator shades and got into the back seat of the car. He then allowed his driver to take him to his next meeting, along with his right-hand man, Tek-9, ready to hold him down.

"Yo, Blanco I don't think it's good to keep this muthafucka around because he might turn on the family in a few months to protect his ass again, feel me?" Tek-9 said.

"I feel you, but I will make sure that doesn't happen because he'll be kept on a close leash," Blanco responded while looking out the window at the New York City streets coming alive with traffic and people everywhere.

CHAPTER 5

Around 1:15 p.m. the next day, Kilo went to the stash house to secure some product for a drop-off over in Queens. Since his homie was hit up, he and the rest of the crew would have to step up and move the product fast, so by the time Young Pablo started to feel better, the money would be ready for him to call his connect down in Little Havana.

Young Pablo's Aunt Maria was in the living room with her friends watching television. The forty-two-year-old redhead was no stranger to the game. She knew her nephew was making money and he paid her well. It was like a family business in which she, too, was involved. Just like the rest of the family, Maria was always strapped with guns and knives in case shit went wrong. But for the most part, people knew not to fuck with their crazy-ass family.

Maria was a killer in disguise hidden behind a sweetheart smile. She stood five foot even and had a light frame. She always wore red lipstick, which was evident when she was near, since she chain-smoked and left behind cigarette butts with a red imprint, tossing them wherever she pleased. Being in this business made her smoke like this, she would always say, since she was always on guard.

Maria sat in the living room talking with her friends about the show they were watching on Univision. Kilo was in the kitchen tucking the bricks into the bag. He was ready to make the move to Queens to get the money.

A knock came across the front door, which was followed by the doorbell ringing. This seemed strange since Maria had put an out-of-order sign on the doorbell. The reason for this was to assure that anyone that did ring the bell would do it in sequence, unlike the manner in which it had just been rung.

She nodded her head to her associate to get up and answer the door. He got up with his MAC-11 in hand that was fully loaded with thirty-two in the clip and one in the chamber. He looked out the peephole and saw two young kids running away.

"Hey, Maria. It's them fucking-ass kids playing that game. What's that shit called?"

"Ring and run. That's when they ring the doorbell multiple times, knock, and then take off, hoping they don't get caught. Remember back in PR, I did that as a kid until I got caught by this old man. He taught me and my crew a lesson. That shit was not funny, I tell you," Maria said, flashing back to her younger days while at the same time making her friends laugh, which broke the tension until the doorbell rang out again. "Kick their little asses!" Maria yelled out, watching as her associate turned back around to get the door.

"Don't worry, Maria. I'll fire a bullet in their ass while they're running away."

He quickly swung the door open ready to scare the young kids, only to be greeted by twin nickel-plated 9 mms staring him in the face and bringing a halt to all of his thoughts, while freezing in the moment as a low-commanding voice spoke.

"You act stupid or move, and you die. I'ma blow your fucking head off. Now back into the house. You already know what this is!" Tek-9 commanded, ready to get at the bricks that Flaco said were inside.

Maria's associate was pissed off that this muthafucka had the drop on him; however, he knew that one false move and his ass was gone.

Tek-9 arrived with two well-known Black Mafia lieutenants, Ali Mo and Flirt, along with two other goons associated with the family.

Ali Mo was a real gangsta born in Harlem and stood five foot eight. He was dark skinned and had a crazy-looking left eye that he received after getting stabbed up north on the yard. This only added to his gangsta stare, and he would lay down any nigga that thought the eye thing was funny. He would show them how much pain was really funny. Ali Mo came through the door with twin Glock 7s war ready and rocked out with extended clips.

Ali Mo's cousin, Flirt, was right behind him with two black-steel snub-nose .44 Magnums. Flirt was also Harlem-born and raised, and he weighed 220 and stood five foot nine. He was a little on the heavy side but went about his business, wearing glasses and a small afro that only added to his ghetto genius look.

They came into the crib fast and had the drop on everyone. Maria became pissed when she saw the muthafuckas come through her house with guns out, especially with her being strapped with a 9 mm Uzi under the pillow on the couch with the safety off. She was ready to unleash the fifty bullets in its clip. She rested her arm on top of the pillow as the other arm was under the pillow holding on to the grip of the gun ready to take out these puntas.

Maria's associate was on the couch across from her and was also strapped with a fully-loaded MAC-10.

The one person Tek-9 focused on was the one that came to the door with the gun in his hand, so he tucked his twin 9 mms into his waist line before snatching the gun from the Latino and turning it on him.

"All of y'all up in here know what it's hitting for! We can do this the easy way or the hard way!" Tek-9 announced, making eye contact with Maria and then the other Spanish nigga on the couch.

He came to do a job, easy or not, which was to get the cocaine and/or money.

Kilo was still in the kitchen loading bricks into the bag when he heard the commotion going on in the front room, so he grabbed his 9mm Ruger off the table with one ready in the chamber. He started quietly creeping toward the living room as his adrenaline started to spike. He knew he was about to put in some work by the sound of the loud voice coming from the front room.

Tek-9 was in the living room and losing his

patience, since none of the Latinos budged from their positions when he demanded them to do so, while indirectly wanting to rob them.

"Where is the fucking cocaine, ma! You know why we here!" Tek-9 snapped while staring at Maria, knowing she of all people would know where the cocaine was located, based on what Flaco had told them.

Maria stared back at him and feared nothing. She wanted to kill him where he stood, but his gun was already in her face now, so she could not afford to move suddenly.

Tek-9 did not want to waste any more time. He saw that these muthafuckas were standing firm, so he shifted his gun back to the Latino that had answered the door. He fired a slug into the back of his head, blowing out skull fragments and chunks of brain from the front of his face. A warm sticky mist sprayed Maria as she sat on the couch watching her good friend be killed in front of her. His body fell limp and lifeless to the floor.

The spraying of the brains saturated Maria's white plush couch, and she even had blood and brain matter sliding down her face, which angered her even more.

"You asshole! You will pay for this, and your blood will be all over the place as I gut you like a pig! You know who we are!" Maria said with fire in her eyes, wanting to kill him right then.

"I don't give a fuck who you are or who you're related to. I came for one thing—the muthafucking cocaine, you stupid bitch!"

As those words flowed from Tek-9's mouth, Kilo swung into the room. At the same time, Flirt saw his quick movement, so he yelled out and squeezed off a round from the thunderous .44 Magnums.

"Yo, look out, nigga!"

Kilo squeezed the trigger and sent slugs through the air, which tracked down and hit one of the two goons standing beside Tek-9.

Right then everything seemed to go in slow motion as bullets were exchanged. The sudden burst of gunfire shifted everyone's attention, which gave Maria the time she needed to remove her weapon. At the same time, she jumped up from her position as things picked up speed, and unexpectedly for Tek-9, she shifted her weapon onto him.

"I told you, fool! I got you, muthafucka!" Maria yelled as she sprayed Tek-9 and dropped him with a barrage of multiple slugs to his body, as his gun followed with him to the floor.

She then gunned down the other goon standing nearby, looking like he was ready to fire on her, but she beat him to it. After dropping him, she tried firing on Ali Mo, but he fired on her first, knocking down her small frame onto the couch and badly wounding her. Tek-9 was on the floor wounded but still feeling the adrenaline in his body to move a little. Flirt squeezed the triggers on the Magnums as he backed out of the house and tried to evade the cross fire. This also allowed him to reload by using the speed loaders.

Ali Mo then focused his rounds on Kilo, who was charging toward him and firing off rounds, until he realized that he had run out. He still ran toward Ali Mo in an attempt to tackle him until he was stopped with a slug to the forehead, which ended all of those thoughts and, at the same time, dropped him in his forward progress. Kilo wanting to hold it down until the end, but he never saw the end come as fast as it did.

The other Latino squeezed off rounds and gunned down Ali Mo, which forced him off his feet. As his body was thrust backward in mid-air, he fired off a few rounds and took out the Latino that had just shot him.

"Muthafucka, you got me! This shit burns!" Ali Mo cried out, feeling the hot slugs eat away at his flesh.

The wounded Tek-9 beside him saw that his homeboy was hit, so he raised up his gun and blasted the Latino, leaving him unrecognizable. In pain, Ali Mo's adrenaline was still flowing, so he got up and made his way over to help Tek-9, who was struggling to get to his feet.

"That's what I'm talking about, my nigga. This is some crazy-ass *Scarface* shit!" Ali Mo said.

"I know, my nigga. That crazy bitch caught me slipping. I knew I should have shot her first," Tek-9 said, thinking Maria was dead.

But she was only wounded, and the slugs had only briefly knocked her unconscious. With all of her might and anger, and wanting revenge on the muthafuckas that had come into her crib, Maria opened her eyes. She jumped up and focused her Uzi on Tek-9, who was trying to stand up, until the roaring burst of gunfire sounded off. The 9 mm Uzi spit out a fire of death as each slug crashed into his body over and over, hitting Ali Mo since he had turned over to block the slugs covering Tek-9. The slugs instantly killed Ali Mo, and the force of the slugs knocked Tek-9 back down. Maria quickly hopped over to him. She wanted to finish him off. Tek-9 tried to raise his gun, since he knew the crazy bitch was coming his way and fast.

"Don't even think about it, motherfucker! You motherfuckers don't know who you're fucking with!"

"Fuck you, you crazy-ass bitch!"

"No! Fuck you, punta!" Maria replied as she spit blood out onto Tek-9 and took aim.

At the same time, Flirt walked in from outside after reloading both Magnums. He squeezed off both Magnums, which sounded off like a dark night of thunder and lightning. Each time he pulled the trigger, he sent unforgiving slugs into Maria's small frame, which thrust her body into the air and killed her before she even hit the ground. The brute force of the slugs even broke her bones on impact.

Flirt was pissed when he saw that his cousin was dead.

"That's for my cousin, you stupid bitch!" Flirt yelled.

"Flirt, help me up, nigga," Tek-9 asked.

He rushed over to him and helped him to his feet.

"Yo, run into the kitchen where that nigga came from, and see what they got up in there. I'll stand here waiting on you."

Flirt followed orders and returned with the bag of cocaine and more that Kilo had ready to go. Then he ran past Tek-9 out to the car, placed the work into the trunk, and returned back into the house to help his friend.

"I thought you forgot a nigga for a minute."

"Nah, nigga, I had to run that shit out to the car. That's fuck up she killed my cousin," Flirt said as they got into his S550 Mercedes Benz, mashed the gas, and left the area.

The people in the hood knew the code of the streets, so they would not be around when the cops arrived.

"Damn, this shit is mad crazy, son! You good back there?" Flirt asked, making sure Tek-9 was all right.

"Yeah, B. I just need to go to the hospital. I'm losing too much blood. I think when she shot Ali Mo, one of them slugs came through and hit me in the ribs, son," Tek-9 said while embracing the pain yet feeling good about the come-up with the bricks.

CHAPTER 6

While the police secured the crime scene at Maria's crib, Young Pablo was still in the hospital watching TV with Gordo, who was holding him down. Pito and Chico ran around and secured the money business to make sure the team stayed in power. They were all unaware that Flaco's slimy ass gave up their stash house that led to Maria and Kilo's deaths.

Young Pablo went into a daze watching television while thinking back to when Flaco had shot him. It angered him, and he wanted revenge on everyone that stood in his way.

"Hey, Gordo, I want Flaco dead. I want his family to wish he was never born," Young Pablo said angrily. "Before we kill him, I want to cut off both his hands for stealing from me. I'll first let him feel that pain, and then blow his fucking brains out!"

"I feel you, bro. We going to track him down and make him pay. As for them Black Mafia muthafuckas, they're going to wish they never did business with him," Gordo said.

Gordo's cell phone sounded off and halted their conversation. He saw that it was his homie, Chico, calling.

"What's up, Chico?"

"The motherfuckers hit our stash house and killed Maria, Kilo, and everybody in the crib!"

Hearing this made Gordo's heart jump when he thought about the loss of his homie, Kilo, as well as the loss of the product and Maria. This act alone meant war.

"How do you know it was them?" he asked,

wanting to confirm this before relaying the info to Young Pablo, who appeared alert to Gordo's tone of voice.

"Because Maria and her team killed a few of them, too, before they were killed."

"Flaco must have told them where our spot is. That piece of shit!" Gordo yelled.

"What's up, Gordo?" Young Pablo questioned anxiously.

"Them motherfuckers hit Maria's spot and killed everyone," he said.

His words stung deep into Young Pablo's flesh, when he began to think about his aunt and how she had raised him in the game and in life. Without question, he would have to respond to this with a wave of gunfire to get the Black Mafia's attention and respect.

"I can't sit back and allow this punta to betray me like this. Them motherfuckers fucked up by killing my family," Young Pablo said, obviously angered by this situation.

He started pulling out the IVs from his arm. He did not want to be in the hospital while all of this was going on. Being here made him feel helpless and powerless, and he needed power to maintain his empire. For him it was not about the cocaine that had been stolen. He could always get that back. But they killed his aunt and homie, and neither one of them could be replaced.

"Chico, meet me at the hospital. Pablo's pulling out his IVs and trying to leave and shit!"

After he hung up the phone, he came over to Young Pablo and helped him back into the bed.

"You can't just leave, bro. You have to be at 100

percent; otherwise, you're no good to yourself or anyone else."

"I'm ready for war now! We have to hit them motherfuckers and Flaco now! I'm not soft, plus they killed my aunt and our homie, Kilo. We can't let this shit go!"

"You know I'ma ride with you no matter what. But right now, you're not in the best condition to do anything. We'll handle this shit before it gets out of control. You have my word."

"Call my sister now! We have to make a move, because that piece of shit, Flaco, and those motherfuckers need to feel my presence and power!"

"Got it. I'll call her right now," he replied.

Cat picked up on the first ring. She was thinking and feeling that something was wrong.

"Gordo, why is it that when you call I get this bad

feeling something is wrong?"

"It's not good. The motherfuckers hit Maria's place and laid down the house, including our homie, Kilo. Your brother wants to see you now."

"I'm on my way."

Catrina was pissed when she heard the news and felt the same disrespect her brother had. They would now have to retaliate with force to display their power. At the same time, they hoped they would force the Black Mafia to turn Flaco over to them.

Flirt took Tek-9 to the same hospital Young Pablo was at, obviously unaware that he was there. The family's doctor left town after dealing with Flaco.

Flirt dropped Tek-9 off at the front door, when he saw a nurse taking a cigarette break. Once he dropped him off, he quickly drove off. He was heavy with the bricks of cocaine they just took, so he could not stick around for the cops to come asking questions.

As he turned the bend to leave the hospital, Kitty Cat and her crew pulled up in her candy-apple-red Lexus 600 with custom chrome flakes, 23-inch chrome rims with candy-apple-red inlay, and matching light-red tinted windows. Cat also saw Flirt rush away from the hospital. She knew he was an associate of the Black Mafia.

She came to an abrupt stop in front of the hospital and could only think about getting to her baby brother. Cat, Mya, and Princess all raced up to the seventh floor in the elevator and made their way to Young Pablo's room. Their hearts beat fast thinking the worst; however, once they made it into his room, they realized everything was okay.

"Baby bro, you good up in here?" Cat asked while still breathing heavy.

Adrenaline had increased her heart rate, and her mind raced while thinking the worst had occurred until she set eyes on Young Pablo.

"I'm good, but why y'all rushing up like that?"

"I saw the guy Flirt, from the Black Mafia leave in a hurry, so I thought he came up in here."

"Nobody knows I'm here. Even so, I can't stay here too long. I'm ready to go to war with them motherfuckers that ran up in my stash house and killed aunty and my homie."

Cat and her girls put their guns away and concealed them in waistlines of their sexy and tight-fitting jeans.

"He wasn't here for Pablo. I think with that shootout over at Maria's, one of them motherfuckers got hit. You know Maria stayed strapped and war ready."

"You're right, Gordo! Maria's a gangsta bitch fo' real," Mya said with her soft-spoken Latina accent.

"Cat, we should go see who Flirt dropped off within the last fifteen minutes with a gunshot-related wound. It shouldn't be that hard to find," Princess stated, ready to put in some work.

"Bro, we're on that now. If someone is here, then we can't stay, but that punta will die here!" Cat said.

"As soon as you're done searching or finding who you're looking for, get back to me, because we have to stay ahead of them motherfuckers," Young Pablo said.

Cat kissed her baby bro on the cheek before leaving the room to take care of business.

"Princess! Mya! Let's go handle this and find out

who we're going to kill after they tell us where Flaco is," Cat said, ready to impose her wrath on the entire Black Mafia and anyone associated with them.

They made their way down to the ER and asked questions that would point them in the right direction. Tek-9 did not want any anesthetic because he wanted to be alert to everything going on around him in case shit jumped off. He wanted to be in and out, but little did he know he was currently being sought after.

Cat easily obtained the room number in which he was resting. She and her girls acted like concerned friends. They also worked their female beauty and magic that led them to the seventh floor where her baby brother was. How convenient! Kitty Cat was ready to get some resolve.

CHAPTER 7

Meanwhile over in Brooklyn, Flirt had just arrived at the warehouse where Blanco was waiting for him to come with the take from the robbery.

Flirt entered the warehouse with a duffle bag full of bricks, plus a few loose bricks in his hand. As he approached, Blanco appreciated the sight of the bricks because he equated them with money. As Flirt closed in, Blanco noticing the blood splatter on his clothing. It then hit him that he had arrived alone, without Ali Mo, Tek-9, or the street goons. The thought that he might have lost men was not good. Even worse, he knew that when the cops discovered dead men on a crime scene connected to the Black Mafia, it would lead back to him. This was not good.

"You coming alone isn't a good sign that it went

well."

"I got the work, so that was the objective. But we lost my cousin, Ali Mo, along with the street goons. You knew like they knew that it wasn't going to be easy going up in there. Flaco was right. Maria was all about her work," Flirt said.

"How much product did you walk out with?" Blanco asked, mainly focused on the cocaine, because this is how he was going to make money for the family.

"Thirty bricks plus what I carried in."

"The money from five of them blocks goes to Ali Mo's family and kids. As long as we out here, the family is going to take care of his kids until they get old enough to join the family," Blanco said, always thinking about investing and making money. "The money from twenty gets flipped back to me for the family's interest. As for what's left, you, Tek-9, and Flaco can split it."

Flaco sat back in the chair as Flirt divided everything up. Blanco was still in thought trying to figure out his next steps.

"Mira, Flaco, your life insurance just went up since we lost a few of my associates," Blanco said. He then added, "I can assure you that more blood will be shed because of your betrayal, but this is where my family comes into play. We protect those that need us."

Flaco now realized he was playing with a double-edged sword by crossing Young Pablo, only to inherit more problems with the Black Mafia. His mind raced while trying to find words to say in order to evade the pressure he was feeling, as Blanco stood waiting on him to say something. Blanco's phone rang, which shifted his attention. Lucky for Flaco, he would now have more time to think his way out of this jam.

Blanco saw that Tek-9 was calling him, so he answered it. He wanted to know how his homie was feeling after being hit up.

"Talk to me."

"Yo, Blanco, it's me, Tek-9, nigga. I'm over here at the hospital. Is Flirt good? Did he make it back to the spot?"

"He good, and your cut is waiting for you, too."

"You know I can't be up in here too long. Them crazy-ass Spanish niggas will be looking for a nigga, feel me?"

"I'll send a few goons over to hold you down until you can leave the hospital. Plus, I'll stop by after I secure things over this way."

"Good looking, my nigga. Oh shit, what the fuck!?" Tek-9 yelled when he saw Cat and her girls walk into his room with strapped guns aimed at him.

"Yo, Tek-9, you good, my nig?"

Cat fired a silenced burst of rounds into his stomach. The force of the slugs abruptly knocked the wind out of him, which caused him to drop his cell phone as he reached for his stomach in pain. Cat grabbed his phone and heard Blanco on the other end calling out for Tek-9.

"You bitches are crazy coming up in here like y'all don't know who I represent!" Tek-9 said while clenching his stomach.

"We know who you are, idiot! How do you think we found you? You fucked up!" Mya said while pressing her gun against his temple.

"Papi can't talk right now. My girl just put her

gun in his mouth," Cat said, talking about Princess. "If he moves, he's dead with no hesitation!" Cat ordered.

"Who the fuck is this?" Blanco screamed.

"La Primera Dame de Calles. You heard of me? Now who am I speaking to?"

"This is Brooklyn Blanco. You know who I am and what I represent!"

"Truthfully, I don't care who you are. But if you want to see your boy again, I think we have to make an exchange."

"What exchange is that?" he asked as if he didn't know what she was talking about.

"First, we can start with the cocaine you guys stole from my brother's stash house. When you bring the product, make sure Flaco is with you; and don't say he's not with you, because I already know he is."

"I can do this. Just give me a time and location."

"Manhattan Club Bed on the second-floor restaurant level in two hours, and don't be late."

"I'll be there on time. I hope I can trust that you'll keep your word."

"My word is all I have, so don't be late," she said before hanging up the phone and tossing it over to Tek-9. "You know I can't let you live after what y'all did to my aunt and friends. Mya, kill this fool so we can get out of here," Cat ordered, giving Tek-9 a murderous stare before turning to walk away.

"My pleasure, mami," Mya agreed, before pumping two silenced rounds into Tek-9's face, snapping his head back with abrupt force and instantly breaking his neck and killing him.

They all raced out of the room when the heart

monitor begin to beep louder and faster as they ran to Young Pablo's room on the other side of the floor.

"Somebody is here, huh?" Young Pablo asked upon seeing the looks on their faces and hearing their fast breathing as they entered the room.

"Yeah, one of their enforcers. He was hit up from robbing the stash house, but we left him behind. But we did secure a meeting with the Black Mafia's underboss," Cat said after catching her breath. "Gordo, help my brother out of the bed and take him to my grandma's spot. Then call up Chico and Pito and have them meet me so we can secure this shit with them motherfuckers."

"I got you, Cat. I'ma handle this over here, so just make sure you take care of your sexy self."

"She's with us, Gordo, so she's always in good hands," Mya said as they rolled out to handle

71

business with the Black Mafia.

Gordo helped Young Pablo out of the hospital and into his black M60 Infinity that was tricked out with 23-inch rims and dark-tinted windows that concealed the TVs throughout.

Once they made it away from the hospital, he called up Chico and Pito and made them aware of what was going down with the Black Mafia as well as the move with Young Pablo, so they wouldn't think he was still at the hospital.

"Gordo, no matter what, we can't let these muthafuckas take us out of the game. We put in too much work to get this far. If my brother takes care of this for me, we'll come out on top, even if we don't get Flaco."

"I feel you, bro. Blood in, blood out. We gonna get this money or die trying, just like fifty said,"

Gordo responded, knowing he would have to stay on point from now on because the Black Mafia was going to come hard when they learned that one of their own had be slain at the hospital.

73

CHAPTER 8

Back over in Brooklyn, Blanco was snapping about how the call went with Catrina. He thought about the meeting with her and how it may have unfolded with gun play. He did not want this problem trickling back to his boss, the number one guy running the family: Cocaine Smitty.

"This bitch was at the hospital with Tek-9 in his room. How the fuck did they know he was there?" he questioned.

Flirt looked on at Blanco as he was venting. He wanted to know what had just taken place, but he just continued on rambling.

"They want this nigga Flaco plus the cocaine in exchange for Tek-9!"

At the sound of having to give the money back,

Flirt's eyebrows raised when he thought about how that was going to work, because he did not want to give up his share.

"Blanco, my cousin got laid out for this shit, feel me? I ain't trying to just give the work back."

"Mira, Blanco, I ain't feeling the part about me being traded either. Fuck the cocaine! You can give them that shit, but I'm not going back."

Flaco, Flirt, and Blanco were all in disagreement about what should take place. Blanco even tried to reason while he was working out things mentally. Tek-9 was still a Black Mafia associate that he was not going to abandon.

"Listen to y'all niggas as if Tek-9 didn't spill blood for this family. So what am I supposed to do, forget about my nigga?" he asked while looking on at them before adding, "This is what we're going to do. Make them think they're getting all of the product back, and make them think we have you waiting to be turned over. We clear on that?"

"Yeah, I'm good, my nig, but we need to round up a team to hold us down when we go meet them. She can't be trusted," Flirt assured.

"Flirt's right, Blanco. This bitch is vicious. For all we know, Tek-9 could already he dead," Flaco said.

"Let's get this shit popping. I want to get the team together so we can go over the strong points, because we can't afford to get caught slipping," Blanco suggested.

"I'll get the little homies in the hood that want to get down with us. They'll do what we tell them."

"All they need to know is that if shit hits the fan, no one leaves the club if it's not us."

"Say no more. I'm all over it 'cause I'm not trying to walk into a trap."

Blanco and Flirt were focusing on making this deal go through, not realizing they were walking into Kitty Cat's trap, even if they did not see it as one. The only thing they saw was disrespect because she had captured one of their own, Tek-9, and held him for ransom. Little did they know he was already dead and long gone.

Flirt and Blanco both were aware of Cat's notable beauty, which was not only alluring but also deceptively luring to both men and women, when she wanted to take them out or use them to her advantage. Neither one of them had ever even seen her in person and never needed to until now.

CHAPTER 9

Two hours had passed by when Blanco, Flirt, and their goons made their way over to Club Bed in Manhattan. Blanco and Flirt were in the underboss's all-white Bentley Flying Spur sitting on 24s.

The Black Mafia associates behind him were in a Lexus 450s strapped with their weapons concealed under their white tees. Flaco stayed back at the warehouse as directed by Blanco. The other associates stood by and waited on call in case they were needed to make a move.

When the car came to a stop, Flirt exited first and looked around to make sure it was clear and safe to get out. He nodded his head and signaled Blanco to get out. He stepped out into the seventy-six-degree New York air and took in a deep breath that seemed to be a little hotter than normal, especially with his adrenaline flowing coupled with the tension of the situation. He slipped his shades on before nodding to his young goons in the cars. Then, four of the young goons exited the car, adjusted their weapons, and walked toward Blanco to see what the underboss had to say.

"I need y'all to follow me and Flirt into the club. The rest of the crew can stay out here and hold us down. Flirt, put them onto what we talked about."

"Nobody comes in or out if you don't see us first."

"Enough said. So let's go meet this pretty bitch!" Blanco said as he made his way over to the entrance.

Once inside the elevator, thoughts of what might happen next came to mind as the young goons pulled out their weapons and stood guard. When the elevator reached the second floor and the doors parted, the four goons stepped out and took positions around the area as Flirt and Blanco stepped out. Flirt noticed the sexy-ass Latina wave them over to the bed, so he tapped Blanco to get his attention as he pointed over in her direction.

"Blanco, I think that's Young Pablo's sexy-ass sister right there."

Blanco made eye contact with the four goons that came in with him and directed them with his head where to go in the restaurant to protect him. Flirt made sure one of them stayed by the elevator just in case shit popped off. He did not want anyone sliding out.

"Flirt, let's go take care of the business we came for."

"Yo, mami looks crazy-sexy in person, B. She

definitely will catch a nigga slipping."

"Stay focused, Flirt. She's the same pretty bitch that will bury you in a heartbeat."

They made their way over to her. She looked seductive on the bed wearing tight red YSL jeans and a white silk Prada top. She had flowing hair, glowing eyes, and an alluring smile with dimples, and she had on diamonds in her ears, around her neck, on her wrist, and in her watch that sparkled as much as her eyes that seemed to lure in most people.

"You two look surprised, as if I'm not what you expected," Kitty Cat said after seeing the expressions on their faces.

Now up close and personal with her, Blanco was able to see the allure that captivated most men and women.

"I guess you can say your beauty doesn't match

your notable reputation."

"Am I to assume that's your way of giving me a compliment?" Cat questioned with a smile before she added, "But you didn't come here for a date or to get to know me on that level. You came to do business. But first allow me to order you guys a drink. What would you two like?"

Neither of them expected her hospitality, since she was really only known for being violent.

"Give me a double shot of Henny. Flirt, what you drinking?"

"Give me a double shot of Peach Cîroc."

Cat turned and signaled the waitress over so she could place the order.

"We need a double shot of Henny, a double shot of Peach Cîroc, and a rum and Coca-Cola."

The prompt server delivered the drinks within

minutes. Blanco and Flirt were not there for drinks or pleasure, so they downed their shots since they wanted to get straight to the point.

"Thanks for the drinks. Now let's deal with the business we came here for. Where's my associate?" Blanco asked, questioning where Tek-9 was.

"He's nearby. Now what about Flaco and the cocaine. Where are they?"

Blanco waved over one of his goons with a bag of cocaine containing ten of the kilos they had taken. The goon set the bag down on the bed beside Cat before going back to his position.

"Here's your cocaine. Now give one something."

"Just a minute. This looks kind of light, Blanco. Where's the rest?"

"I give you a little and you give me a little, mami. You know how this thing works."

"Hey, Blanco, the cocaine is a small factor in this whole negotiation. My sole interest is getting Flaco back. He has some unfinished business with my brother. So did you bring him or not?"

Blanco could not see past her beauty and more toward the business side of this violent bitch. He knew she was not going to just let this go easily. As he was about to respond, his cell phone sounded off and got his attention. When he answered the phone, he started to feel a bit light-headed.

"What's up? Who's this?"

"Blanco, this is Flaco. ! It's a setup! It's all over the news that Tek-9 got slumped in his hospital room. That bitch is up to something!"

"What? Wha?"

Blanco's heart and mind raced with this new information.

He was ready to snap on Cat as he hung up the phone. But just as he was about to reach for his gun, he was unable to do so because the sedative in his drink had made him dizzy, weak, and confused, and his vision became blurred. It forced him to sit down on the edge of the bed, and he then knew something was wrong.

"You fucking bitch! You put something in our drinks!"

He became unconscious as those words flowed from his mouth.

Cat laid him beside her and looked over at Mya and Princess, who were blending in with the rest of group inside the restaurant. Flirt tried to reach for his gun, until the serum kicked in and shut down all of his movements, dropping him onto the floor. Suddenly, Princess and Mya took out the other goons standing by with silenced rounds that they never even saw coming. Cat called Pito and alerted him to the next step in the trap she had set up for Blanco and his team.

"Pito, it's time for you to do your thing."

Pito and a few of his Spanish Harlem goons came through on tricked-out custom-painted Kawasaki Ninjas. They were ready for war. Pito saw that three of the Black Mafia associates were still sitting in the car, while the other stood outside smoking a cigarette.

Pito rode up on his motorcycle and came to a stop right beside the Lexus, reached down to the compartment of his bike, took out a grenade, and tossed it back out. But it was too late. The blast came faster than they expected, tearing through their flesh, sucking the life from their bodies, and instantly killing them. The one goon standing outside the car smoking also caught some of the shrapnel, as his body was tossed away from the car wounding him. He was left in shock from the unexpected blast.

Pito turned around and saw the lone goon wounded and moving around in pain, so he raced back over to him and pulled out his Glock 40 from his pant leg. He came up on the Black Mafia goon and fired off two rounds into his head, which left him no chance of survival. The civilians in the area stayed low after hearing the blast and then the gunfire. They did not want to witness these two organizations going to war. Pito called up Cat and made her aware that he had secured the front.

"Cat, it's go time."

"We're on our way," she responded after having paid off Latino thugs from the hood to bring Flirt's and Blanco's unconscious bodies down to the awaiting cargo van.

"All right, we got this from here, ma. We'll meet you at the spot," Pito said.

Blanco and Flirt never saw it coming, because they were expecting violence. Instead, they were deceived by her hospitality that led them to drink from the cups of deception, sending them into a dark sleep, while she arranged for them to be taken to a secured location and have control over them until they gave her what she needed: Flaco.

Cat and her girls jumped into Mya's baby-blue Audi S8 with the V10 engine and chrome 23s with her name engraved in the center of them. She mashed the gas, raced away from the club area, and blended into the New York streets. While they were in motion, Cat called up her baby bro to let him know what had just taken place.

"What's up, brother, you good?"

"Yeah, you?"

"Yeah, they tried to play us by not bringing that piece of shit, and then they came short with the product, which was another sign of disrespect. But I was already one step ahead of them motherfuckers. I now have the underboss and their lieutenant, so if the boss of this family doesn't turn Flaco over to me, I'll kill them both."

"They asked for this, so now they have to deal with the problem of protecting that piece of shit. They want war and we'll give it to them. One thing, Cat, we can't lose focus of getting the money."

"Money is always on my mind, you know this. As for those motherfuckers, now they know who they're fucking with. I should have Flaco by the end of the day; if not, then I'll cut off the underboss's head and send it to the boss to see if Flaco is really worth the cost."

"Call me this afternoon, Sis."

"As soon as I get some answers!" Cat replied before hanging up the phone and thinking about her next step and what she needed to do to get resolve in this situation.

CHAPTER 10

It didn't take long before Cat had the team meet
up at another one of Young Pablo's stash houses,
where they had taken Flirt and Blanco. They had
secured them to chairs and blindfolded them so they
would not know where they were, which was another
advantage Cat had since the men were unconscious.
This psychological advantage gave her the edge she
needed to get through to them.

"Pito and Chico, I appreciate how y'all held it
down over there at the club. Now that we have these
two puntas, they have to give us Flaco. I hope their
boss will see it the same way!" Cat hoped.

"Even though we got some of the work back,
someone has to pay for the loss of Maria and Kilo,"
Pito announced.

"Pito, right, mami," Mya said, looking over at Flirt and Blanco secured to chairs. "Where are their phones? We can get straight to it. Flaco in exchange for them."

"Here are their phones. I already ran their pockets and took their money. They ain't going to need it," Chico said as Mya started going through their phones in search of important contact number.

"Pito, whose phone is this one?" Mya asked.

"It's that asshole Flirt's."

She didn't want to go through his phone since he would have to answer to Blanco being the number two guy. However, Blanco had to answer to the boss himself.

"What's up with you, mami? What are you

looking for?" Kitty Cat asked Mya.

"He's the number two guy, so he has to answer to someone," Mya said, swiping through all of the numbers until she came to a number that read #1 C-Smitty. Mya saw this and felt it had to be the boss.

"Cat, what do they call that asshole in charge?"

"Cocaine Smitty!" Chico blurted out. "Yeah, he was in the news last year when the Feds thought they had something on him."

"Good looking, papi. Well, here's the number, mami. I think you should be the one to make the call," Mya suggested as she handed her the cell phone.

Cat took the phone but waited before she made the call. She wanted to make a full impact on these muthafuckas.

Cocaine Smitty was a powerful figure in New York who was known and respected in the underground world and made a name for himself growing up. The six-foot-two, 230-pound Mafioso was only thirty-six years of age, but he had seen a lot in his time in the streets. He was also very book smart, which gave him a business edge to organize one of the most lucrative Black-associated outfits as well as import/export distribution companies that allowed the family not only to generate money, but also import illegal goods that made millions for them each month. The family also owned clubs, apartment buildings, car lots and rental services, escort services, and more that empowered the family to compete with other organizations. Their worth and power got the attention of the Italian Mafia with whom they had a mutual relationship in business that allowed everyone to eat.

Cocaine Smitty was a businessman first, whether in the streets or in his office in Harlem. If someone did not pay their dues, then their life would be on the line.

Cat wanted to wake up Flirt and Blanco before she made the call to Cocaine Smitty, so she slapped Flirt with a hard open hand that stung his face.

"What the fuck! Who just slapped me like they're ready to die?" Flirt snapped, unable to see since his eyes were covered.

"Shut the fuck up, punta! You're not in the

position to hurt anyone, let alone kill them. If anyone is going to die today, it's going to be you and your boss here!" Catrina threatened.

Princess came up behind Blanco, took her pistol, and slapped him on the side of his face, which immediately woke him up in pain.

"You asshole, I'm going to kill all you bitches! You think this Black Mafia shit is just a name? We'll wipe all of you muthafuckas out!" Blanco snapped.

"Like Cat, fool, we're the only ones doing the killing today!" Princess said, and then added, "Who you are and what you represent isn't going to help you right now, unless you give us what we came for."

"Cat, let me kill this one right here since he thinks he's the one that has the balls in this room!" Mya begged while she walked up to him and pointed her pistol into his groin "You think you got balls? I don't feel nothing here!" Mya added.

"Mya, don't shoot him yet. We have business to take care of!" Cat began. "Remove their blindfolds so they can see what's going on. You two idiots wouldn't be in this position if you would have just brought Flaco along. Like I said, the cocaine is a small factor in this equation," she reminded them as she raised up the phone from her side to call Cocaine Smitty. "Now it's time we reached out to your boss to see if he can give us better resolve than you and Flirt."

"You stupid muthafucka! Cocaine Smitty will storm the streets of Spanish Harlem killing anyone associated with you and Young Pablo!"

Pito did not like what he was hearing Blanco say, so he aggressively shoved his gun into the back of his head.

"You dumb muthafucka, ain't nobody coming into our hood with beef unless they want to die!" Pito snapped.

He pulled back from unleashing slugs into Blanco. He then made eye contact with Cat, who nodded her head for him to step to the side.

"Back to business!" Cat said as she tapped the screen to call Cocaine Smitty.

Cocaine Smitty was in the Bronx sitting outside an Italian deli and enjoying freshly sliced Boar's Head ham, aged cheese, olives, and Italian bread that had been baked that morning. It was crisp but full of flavor, especially if dipped into the olive oil and eaten with the ham and cheese.

Cocaine Smitty was in the presence of the deli owner and made man Paul "Pauly Fingers" Clericuzio, a capo of the family run by Don Michael Clericuzio. Pauly Fingers was fifty years old and stood five foot nine. He was well groomed with combed-back graying hair that displayed his wisdom, as he would say. His thick eyebrows added to his murderous dark stare that went along with his New York Italian accent that always seemed commanding.

Pauly was always about business. He was a man of his word when it came to taking care of business.

He was also known for cutting guys' fingers off to get information from them. Once he got the info, he would kill them and shove their fingers down their throats, just to get his point across.

Pauly became acquainted with Smitty several years back when Pauly found out that his nephew, Donte, was doing business with the Black Mafia. They had a strong bond since their business evolved. The two were enjoying their lunch and conversation before Smitty's cell phone sounded off.

"One second, Pauly, I have to take this. It's my number-two guy," Cocaine Smitty said while getting up from the table.

"No problem, Smitty. Ya gotta do whatcha gotta do, ya know. I'm going to eat the rest of this food over here."

Smitty answered the phone and assumed that it was Blanco, but to his surprise, a female voice came back over the phone.

"Where's Blanco?" he asked, thinking it was one of his side chicks checking his phone.

"He can't come to the phone right now, papi. He's tied up. But I am glad you answered, because your family has something that belongs to my family. I'm talking about Flaco, a two-face punta that betrayed my brother."

Hearing this information made Cocaine Smitty pissed off because he had never heard of Flaco.

"Why is this Flaco you speak of my concern?" he asked while pacing back and forth.

"He's being protected by your family, and your men robbed close to forty blocks from our spot, and laid my family down in the process. So now I have Blanco and Flirt tied up, and I'm looking for some resolve to this matter. Since you're the one in command, get me some resolve!"

Cocaine Smitty had no knowledge of Blanco's protection of Flaco, because he did not even know Flaco. All he knew was that Blanco brought in money for the family.

"Identify yourself, bitch, because I want to know who I'm going to kill after this phone call!" he voiced aggressively while feeling disrespected since she said she had his two guys tied up.

"Papi, you're not in control right now, so lower

your tone of voice. As for who I am, I'm La Primera Dama de Calles, and don't for one second think I won't kill your men and then come for you, especially if you can't give me what I want."

Smitty was pissed and gritting his teeth while processing his thoughts on the shit she was saying. But at the same time, he felt disrespected. He was more angry with his number-two guy for not making him aware that the family was being used as a shield for Flaco, a person he did not know or never even met.

"Yo, ma, I don't know what you're talking about since my number two guy doesn't have to inform me of every little detail, but I will get to the bottom of this. I'll call you back within the hour."

"Just in case you think this shit isn't real, listen up," Cat said, placing her gun to Flirt's leg and firing off a round.

She broke the bone as the brute force of the slug burned and inflicted pain on him.

"Aaagggh! You crazy-ass bitch! I can't wait to kill yo' ass! What the fuck is wrong with you?"

"Nothing is wrong with me, but there will be something wrong with you if your boss doesn't make this shit right!" Cat admitted.

Cocaine Smitty could hear his lieutenant scream in the background. He wanted to say something, but Catrina hung up the phone and left him to think about his next move before he called her back.

After the call, Pauly Fingers became curious to

know if his associate was okay.

"Aye, you don't look so good over there. Is everything all right?" Pauly Fingers asked.

Cocaine Smitty knew that a man of weakness was a liability in the game, so he did not want to show a man of power like Pauly Fingers that he had a problem that could not be dealt with.

"I have to go take care of some things with my family before it gets out of hand."

Pauly chomped down on his sandwich as he stood from the table and sipped his lemonade to chase down the sandwich.

"Aye, you know if you need my assistance with anything I have guys that take care of business, if you know what I mean?" Pauly said before wiping his mouth.

"I'm good, Pauly. I think I can handle this one, but I'll call you later with the details."

Cocaine Smitty turned to his two goons and nodded his head as they made their way over to the all-white Rolls Royce Phantom. After opening the door for his boss, one of the men sat behind the driver's seat. Once Smitty was in the car, the remaining goon got into the front seat, ready to secure and take the boss wherever he pleased.

CHAPTER 11

Cocaine Smitty sat comfortably in the back seat of the Rolls Royce looking on at his cell phone, thinking about his call with Catrina.

"I can't believe these stupid muthafuckas are running around here doing side deals that seem to backfire in their faces! I feel like I need to baby sit these muthafuckas! Do y'all know about this Spanish nigga Flaco being protected by Blanco and his soldiers?"

"Nah, boss, we haven't heard anything about it, but I'll call the others now and see what they know," the goon in the passenger seat replied.

"Handle that call now. I want to know who all is

in on this. They got some explaining to do, especially since I haven't seen a dime of this protection money or side deals these muthafuckas are doing!"

As they continued driving through the streets of New York, the goon called around to other associates to see what they knew, if anything at all. Cocaine Smitty looked out the window and thought about how he was going to handle this situation by making examples out of those involved.

"Boss, I just spoke to the soldiers over in Brooklyn. They're watching over that Flaco nigga right now at the warehouse under Blanco's orders."

"Take me there now," he said while still gritting his teeth.

He wanted to punish someone for the bullshit that

was compromising the Black Mafia.

It did not take long before they arrived at the warehouse, and they made their way to the lounge area off from the offices. Cocaine Smitty got straight to it and saw the soldiers standing around with a lieutenant also present.

"Who the fuck gave the go-ahead to bring this muthafucka into my family and cause all these problems?"

"Uh, boss, uh. He wanted to get money in my hood, so I got at Blanco about this. He arranged a percentage for the family from what Flaco was bringing in, so the family could be happy."

"Happy? Muthafucka, do I look happy?" Smitty said all heated because he was out of the loop on the deal and money was not being sent to him. Blanco was also not there to address the money side of things, but he would have to explain himself and show the money that was not being sent to the boss.

"You started all of this shit, huh, using my family to protect you like you the muthafucking pope or something!" Cocaine Smitty yelled while staring at Flaco with fire in his eyes. He then pulled out his black-steel snub-nose .357 Magnum with hollow-point tips. He rested his finger against the trigger ready to cancel the muthafucka. "Now give me one reason why I shouldn't leave you here stinking. They want you back, but they didn't say how."

Flaco was taken by surprise at this sudden shift in power by having to face the boss. He figured that this meant shit had gone wrong at the club. Now he had to come up with something fast before Smitty killed him or took him back to Young Pablo and his old team. Suddenly, a light clicked on inside his head, and he realized that every man's motivation was money.

"I can tell you where Young Pablo keeps his money, plus I know where everybody lives."

"Now this is what the fuck I'm talking about. He provides under pressure!" Smitty said, lowering his gun. "Give my guys this info. If you're lying, I'll cut your fucking head off and mail it to that crazy bitch that wants you so bad."

"My life is on the line, so I'm not lying. I need money, too, so I can get up out of here for good!"

Flaco said.

He took Flaco up on his proposal and now felt good about receiving all their home addresses as well as where their money house was located. He called up Catrina with this newfound information.

"What's up? Tell me something good."

"I got good and bad news. The good news is that I found Flaco. I figured out what's going on, which is crazy. But the bad news is also good news for me, but bad for you and your whole team."

"What the fuck are you talking about, fool?"

"I know where everybody lives now, so trust me on this one. If we don't come to an understanding quick, I will kill all of you rice-and-bean-eating muthafuckas!"

"Watch your mouth, punta! Another thing, I'm still in control. I told you that before! Hey, look at me, motherfuckers!" Cat said to Blanco and Flirt.

She came up fast on Flirt and fired off a slug into his face, which thrust his entire body back and flipped the chair from the force of the slug. His brains ejected out the other side and left him dead before the chair and his body had hit the floor. The roar of the gun and the sight of his lieutenant being slumped in front of him shocked Blanco, who had a front-row seat to Kitty Cat's violent streak.

"Oh shit! Smitty, this bitch is crazy for real! She just killed Flirt! Come kill all of these muthafuckas! No mercy!"

Cocaine Smitty heard his underboss's pleas,

which forced him to react fast in the situation with force and violence. On the other hand, Cat was feeling the rush of murder after slumping Flirt. It was almost as if she got off on this shit, yet at the same time she embraced the power she got from it.

"Now do we have a better understanding, you fried-chicken-eating bitch!"

"You dumb-ass whore! There will be no negotiations for Flaco other than for your own life in exchange for those you killed!"

Cat was fed up with the back-and-forth small talk and idle threats, so she cut him off and got right to it.

"You right, asshole! No more need for negotiations!"

She then paused and raised her gun to fire on

Blanco. Smitty could hear him in the background yelling out.

"You can kill me, but the Black Mafia will live on, and you will die a thousand times over! One by one, we'll bury all of you bitches!" Blanco yelled out, knowing the end was near.

"Your time is now, punta!" Cat said as she fired off two thunderous slugs into his face, which snapped his neck as the force of the slugs breached his skull and spewed and sprayed his brains and chunks of his skull out the other side. His body and chair fell right beside Flirt's lifeless body.

"Now, Smitty, I'm coming for you!" Cat said before hanging up and leaving him with that thought. She was now ready for war. "Pito! Chico! Take these bodies to Brooklyn and put them in a dumpster so we can make our presence felt. When y'all done, hit me up, because we have to be war ready."

CHAPTER 12

Cocaine Smitty laid low for the past three weeks. Although it was hard to find him directly, he still commanded his family's hits against the Puerto Ricans in Spanish Harlem as well as those against Young Pablo and his sister. At the same time, Cat kept her promise to track down Smitty so she could put a bullet in his head. Young Pablo's team was still holding it down, even though a few street goons had gotten laid out during the rising war between them and the Black Mafia.

One thing both organizations had in common was that they were no longer pulling in the money they were before financing this war. All the drive-by homicides brought the cops into the hoods, which greatly slowed down the pace of the paper chase.

Young Pablo was now able to move around as he pleased with only a little stiffness in his upper body, but he was at least now able to run his empire again. He did not stay in one location too long for security reasons. Cocaine Smitty put out a $250,000 hit on him and his sister, so the streets were gunning for them.

Today he was over at his little mami's crib that he was smashing on the low. She was definitely a ride-or-die gal and would do whatever he asked of her. Gordo also rocked out with him and stayed strapped to make sure his homie was good at all times.

Young Pablo sat in the living room and watched *Shottas*, which was a real gangsta movie with Jamaican niggas.

His little mami came into the living room and

handed him a plate of seasoned pork chops, yellow rice, beans in gravy, fried plantains, and an ice-cold Colt 45 malt liquor to chase it all down.

Gordo walked through the door after taking care of some business. Being a fat boy, he immediately smelled the Latin soul food in the air.

"Damn, bro, that shit smells good. I hope y'all left some for me!"

Rosita walked into the living room with a plate for Gordo.

"Here you go, papi. I know you hungry as always," she said before going back into the kitchen to put together a plate for herself.

He took a bite of the pork chop. He loved it as the flavor burst over his taste buds.

"Damn, Rosita, you did your thing on this, mami."

"Gordo, you know I always put it down. Why you think Pablo keeps coming back?"

"That's between you, him, and the bedroom, mami. Now as for the food, I fucks with this right here," he said as she continued walking back into the kitchen.

Young Pablo continued eating and enjoying his food before taking a moment to discuss family business.

"Hey, Gordo! We have to figure out something with these Black Mafia niggas because it's costing us a lot of money and people."

"I'm here 'til the end, bro. You know business will pick up after this all clears. As for Flaco, he's dead on sight. This Smitty nigga, he ain't gonna give up."

"I was thinking about that. The only way to end

this is murder, but who's going to be first? That's the question."

Gordo stopped eating his food for a moment, leaned back in his chair, and looked at his boss/homeboy. He knew he never backed down from anybody, but he did appear as if he really wanted to end this war and get back to making the money everyone involved was losing.

"It's whatever, bro. You want to send word to this nigga, then do it! Maybe we'll all come to an agreement that makes sense. Real dollars and cents," he suggested, before he then leaned up to his plate and took another bite of the pork chop, followed by a little rice-and-bean gravy that melded all the flavors together.

Young Pablo saw his boy dig deeply into the food, as if he had not eaten all day, and he started to laugh.

"Slow down, fool! Ain't nobody gonna steal that shit from you!" Young Pablo laughed, until he saw someone move past the front window. That caught his attention.

He reached for this MAC-10 with a fifty-round clip. When Gordo saw his buddy make a move, he stopped eating and grabbed hold of his AK-47 with a fifty-round clip. It was already loaded with two clips that were duct taped for quick reload.

Rosita came out from the kitchen and saw both men strapped and war ready. Young Pablo held up his index finger to signify to her to remain quiet before he gestured toward the steps. Without question, she headed upstairs to her bedroom to retrieve the AR-15 that he had bought her the previous week that was fully loaded and ready to go.

Young Pablo crept over to the window and tried to see out. He nudged the curtain just enough to see two Yukon Denalis parked out in front. He also noticed four Black Mafia associates approach with their guns out and ready. He turned to Gordo to put him on to what he had just viewed.

"Mira, they must have followed you back here. There are about six or eight guys spread out, but four of them are coming toward the door now," Young Pablo whispered.

"Damn, my fault, bro. I drove around for a while before I came back here. Fuck it, bro! You know we got to take these fools out."

"I got the door. You take the window."

"Let's kill these motherfuckers."

Young Pablo went to the front door, swung it open fast, and caught them off guard. He squeezed the trigger and gunned down three of the goons that had approached the house. The fourth goon turned quick and took cover, at the same time the other Black Mafia goons revealed their positions and returned fire. Young Pablo was forced back into the doorway as he took cover from the oncoming slugs.

Gordo sprayed AK-47 slugs out the window that crashed into the truck and slumped the get-away driver over the steering wheel.

Young Pablo still covered the front door and was ready to gun down anyone that tried to come through the door. Rosita was now at her bedroom window taking aim at the goons that approached. She began to shoot off bursts of fire from the AR-15.

They all seemed to take cover. The gunfire ceased briefly, and Young Pablo took that time to yell out of the house as he fired rounds in between his sentences.

"You motherfuckers thought it was going to be easy, huh? I ain't going out like that! You fucked with the wrong one!"

He fired off more rounds at the awaiting trucks behind which the goons ran.

"Come on out, muthafucka! You think you're tough! I'm tougher. You want war! I'm built for this war shit!"

Gordo saw that the goons were hiding behind the trucks, so he started walking outside with the AK-47 in front of him. It was loaded and ready to go to war. Young Pablo was right behind him, and they both opened fire on the trucks.

"Toma! Toma! Toma! You don't want war!" Gordo yelled out as he ran down on the last goon with his hands up. He obviously did not want to be shot after he realized he was outgunned and without his team. "Oh no, it's too late for that shit. You came for war. Now here it is!" Gordo explained before firing off a burst of slugs that pounded into his chest and tore through his heart killing him instantly.

"Yo, Pablo, we have to leave this spot now!" Gordo yelled, all ready to go.

"Papi, there's more coming!" Rosita yelled out as she pointed out the window down the street.

At the same time, they could see what she was able to see from the second floor. Another Yukon quickly turned the corner with Black Mafia soldiers hanging out the window with fully automatic weapons. Young Pablo squeezed the trigger on his MAC-10 and sprayed the approaching truck until he heard the clicking sound of his gun that informed him it was empty.

"Hey, Gordo, I gotta reload my shit. It's on the table."

"I got this, bro. Go ahead!"

Gordo started to spray the AK-47 toward the truck, which shattered the front windshield and caused the driver to swerve recklessly while trying to evade the oncoming slugs being fired. The shooter hanging out of the truck was still firing off shots that came through the air, tracking down Gordo and twisting his body as a slug crashed into his shoulder. The other slug found his leg and dropped him. In fear of dying, his adrenaline soared through his body, and he jumped back up. Rosita yelled out from the window for him to get up in between firing her AR-15 at the truck.

"Gordo, you good?"

"I'ma have to be good for now, mami. I don't

have time for anything else. It's time for war!" he yelled out to her while taking aim at the truck.

Young Pablo ran out fast after hearing Rosita yell out for Gordo.

"I got ya back, bro!" Young Pablo said, snapping as he started spraying the MAC-10 when he saw the goons were trying to close in on Gordo.

He quickly gunned down a few of them.

"Don't be trying to die on me, bro!" Young Pablo said to Gordo.

"This ain't about nothing, bro. I'm too pumped up to feel the pain."

"Let's make these fools pay for this shit!" he said as they started moving in on the goons trying to take cover.

They suddenly heard a loud scream from a female inside the truck that caught their immediate attention. The doors of the truck opened followed by a goon escorting a sixteen-year-old girl with a gun to her head as he gripped her ponytail. Gordo snapped when he saw that it was his sister.

"You must have a death wish fucking with my family!"

"You take another step, and I'll leave this little bitch's brains all over the streets!"

"You kill her, and all of you motherfuckers will die just like your homeboys on the ground!"

"We came to die, muthafucka!"

Gordo's sister was scared and feared the worst, that her life was going to come to an end. She did not understand why she was in this position, which made her even more hysterical as she pleaded to be set free.

"Gordo, help me, please! I don't want to die!"

"You're not going to die, sis. This muthafucka

holding you is going to die!"

"I got your back, bro, especially if they hurt your sister. I'll kill 'em all," Young Pablo said, aiming at the goon with the girl.

Time seemed to slow down, as the seconds that passed by seemed like hours. Suddenly, the pounding hearts and heavy breathing were interrupted when two unmarked police cars turned the corner with tires screeching and red-and-blue lights flashing. This was followed by blaring sirens that shifted everyone's attention. Young Pablo took advantage of the moment and fired a burst of rounds into the goon holding Gordo's sister. The blood sprayed onto the young girl, which traumatized her even more, before she took off running toward her brother.

At the sound of gunfire, the other Black Mafia associates opened fire. At the same time, the detectives jumped out of their cars and demanded that everyone drop their weapons. Now the Black Mafia goons focused their weapons on the cops.

Gordo's sister ran toward her brother as he gunned down the Black Mafia associates. But a slug from one of the detective's guns came through the air fast, taking down his sister, ripping through her small frame and puncturing her lung. She fell right in front of Gordo, at his feet, with a look of pain and fear in her young, innocent eyes. Right then he stopped shooting and dropped to his knees to see if his baby sister was okay. But her eyes showed distance as her lungs were filling with her own blood and drowning her.

"Sis! Wake up! Keep your eyes open!" he said, not accepting that she was now gone as her last breath came with her last step toward him. "No!

Noooooo! You muthafuckas killed my sister! Nooooooo!"

Young Pablo saw Gordo go down and thought he was hit again, until he saw Gordo's sister's bloody body. At that moment he, too, could feel his homeboy's pain.

"No mercy! It's all-out war time!" Young Pablo yelled as he sprayed toward the cops and Black Mafia and gunned down as many as he could.

Even Rosita started spraying at the cops when she saw Gordo holding his sister's lifeless body as the gunfire erupted around him.

The unmarked cops came with hopes of running into an easy shakedown. These were crooked cops, and that's what they did. They did not call for back-up, because they thought it would be an in-and-out situation, which was a big mistake on their behalf.

Rosita called up Cat before she returned to let out shots through the air from the second-floor window.

"Papi, your sister is on her way!"

Within a minute or so, Cat, Mya, and Princess arrived on custom pink-and-chrome Katanas and Ninjas. Pito and Chico drove up on 1300cc Hayabusa bikes with gun mounts on the sides for easy access. The detectives were quickly alerted by the sounds of the revving motorcycles, but their focus was still on the Black Mafia goons shooting at them.

Gordo now stood to his feet and wiped away the tears from his face as he took his AK-47 and ran toward the goons. He thought of nothing else other than killing the rest of the Mafia members as well as the cops. He gunned one of them down.

"Take that, muthafucka! That's for my sister, asshole!" Gordo said, enraged.

But being blinded by the moment, he did not see the Black Mafia soldier come around the truck with a 12-gauge shotgun, until he heard the pump action. It was too late.

The trigger pulled delivered multiple buck shots with immense force that lifted Gordo's 240-plus-pound frame from the ground with ease and thrust him back, causing him to release his AK-47 at his feet. In the split second his body left the ground, his entire life flashed before him. His eyes were wide open when he hit the ground. Time seemed to slow down as blood oozed from his mouth and wounds. He blinked a few timed when he realized he was at the end of his life, but at least he would be closer to his baby sister. Young Pablo's screams faded by the second as life slipped away and escaped from his flesh.

Young Pablo gunned down the last two goons. He was enraged that his homeboy had just gotten slumped. He walked over to the downed goons and pumped more slugs into their heads, just to finish them off gang-land style.

"You fucking motherfuckers! I told you, we built for this shit!"

He then shifted his attention to the detectives who by now had called for back-up after they realized that they were outgunned. Cat and the crew unleashed multiple slugs onto the cops. She wanted to get her baby brother out of there. The detectives tried to hold them off, but there were too many guns being fired in their direction. They were killed off one by one, until they came upon the last detective pleading for his life.

"You're all going to jail for this. I'm a fucking

cop, not some gang member!"

"You should have thought about that before you came here; besides, I can't let my baby bro be arrested or ID'd for this shit. You know how this works. You put yourself into this position, and I'm going to help you get out of it," Kitty Cat explained, before firing off a round into the detective's face, leaving him where he stood.

The group did not waste any time getting back onto their bikes ready to roll out. Young Pablo jumped onto Cat's bike. She revved the engine before she took off fast, with the crew right behind her. Young Pablo briefly looked back at his downed homie. He was pissed that this shit had to end like this. Now he wanted to go even harder on the Black Mafia for the loss of his homie.

CHAPTER 13

The police arrived fast after receiving a call of officers down. The sight that they were all greeted with was a gang-land-style massacre. They were all taken by surprise, and their emotions rose for the downed officers. Each of them wished they could have gotten there in time to save their lives, but it was far too late now. It did not take long before homicide detectives showed up. Detective Marlon Johnson was a forty-two-year-old African-American born and raised in New York. He stood five foot ten, weighed 220 pounds, and had a medium build. He had seen a lot in his years on the force as a detective, but nothing like this. There were multiple officers slain from a shootout between two organizations. The dead detectives' wives and children would now have to learn that their loved ones would never return.

"Listen up, people, I want this entire area taped off! I want everybody you see standing around here questioned. Somebody knows the shooters other than the dead ones—the ones that are no longer here. We need to find our killers now!" Detective Johnson yelled out full of emotion.

Detective Johnson knew the Black Mafia associates were sent to take care of business and this was the end result. He also knew the boss of the family because they were from the same hood. They had each just chosen different paths.

Detective Wilson was Johnson's partner and stood six foot even and weighed a slim 190. He had a clean-shaven face with brown hair and favored Johnny Depp. Wilson was a real by-the-book detective. He and Johnson had been partners for close to four years, closing many cases together. They always had each other's back, especially when out in the field.

"Wilson, let's go! It's time we pay an old friend a visit. Someone I haven't seen in a long while. I got a strong feeling he may have the answers we need regarding this massacre here!" Detective Johnson said while getting into his car.

"Are you sure about this? Because we got bodies all over the place here and close to a thousand rounds fired."

"Don't worry, Wilson. These guys can handle it. Besides, the crime scene guys will process it, and then we'll take it from there."

Wilson got into the car and took another glance over at the dead bodies of the downed officers. It bothered him to know that he would now have to track down these killers, and going to jail might be their last choice if his emotions were in the way of justice.

"We'll get these sons of bitches, Wilson. They'll rot upstate or get the death penalty."

"I agree, that could have easily been one of us if we would have answered the call or been in the neighborhood."

He drove off to Brooklyn where he figured he would find Cocaine Smitty. Detective Johnson also was fully aware of his position of power, as well as his connections with the Italian Mafia. Johnson could have easily been a part of this lifestyle had he chosen that path. He may have even been the underboss instead of Blanco, since he had known Cocaine Smitty longer. But he chose to be a cop, working paycheck to paycheck, and he never had to look over his shoulder for the cops or have to face a prison sentence. He may not be making millions like his old friend, but the life he was living made sense to him. He took things one day at a time.

CHAPTER 14

Close to two hours passed by as Detectives Johnson and Wilson drove around Brooklyn in search of Cocaine Smitty, until they got word he may be over in the Bronx. They then headed over to Pauly Fingers's deli where their CI had told them he usually hung out. When their car pulled up to the sidewalk Italian deli, he saw his old friend sitting at the table laughing and enjoying his food and conversation. Smitty was secured by four Black Mafia soldiers dressed in suits that concealed their sidearms. Pauly Fingers was also at the table discussing the problems Smitty was having with Young Pablo's crew.

"So this thing with them Puerto Ricans over there, you have that under control?"

Smitty was surprised Pauly had caught wind of the beef he was having, even though he would have told him personally once things calmed down. Without him even mentioning it, it was clearly a problem. Of course, he did not want Pauly to think there was a problem, because he knew it made guys get paranoid when they thought problems could not be controlled. People start getting whacked, and this is not a good look.

"I have everything under control. Besides, my crew will wipe them all out one by one if they don't submit."

Pauly took a sip of his lemonade when he spotted the fast-approaching detective car. Smitty looked at Pauly's eyes shift, so he turned to see what he was looking at. He recognized Johnson but not Wilson. Both Mafia goons stayed seated until the detectives came over and flashed their badges. The Mafia associates from Smitty's and Pauly's crews stopped both detectives.

"It's okay, guys, let them pass. They know what's good for them, if they start acting crazy. Besides, they're here to entertain us," Pauly Fingers said.

Detective Wilson seemed a bit nervous when the Mafia goons brought them to a halt. On the other hand, his partner simply walked over to the table.

"Do you mind if I have a seat?" Johnson asked while sitting down without waiting for a response.

"State your business, Detective, because your

presence isn't exactly good for my business, you know?" Pauly stated in a commanding yet mild tone.

"My business is that I have four dead detectives murdered gang-land style, along with eight black males and two dead Latinos over in Spanish Harlem. The dead brothers are from your crew," Detective Johnson said, while staring at Cocaine Smitty, who did not flinch one bit as he stared back at the detective through his Sean Jean aviators. "Dead cops mean no money will be made until we get someone to fall for this!"

Smitty did not care about what the cop said or his attempt to put pressure on him about this matter. What he did care about was how he was being disrespected in front of his friend and made man

Pauly Fingers.

"Help me understand, Detective. You come here and interrupt my dinner that I'm having with a good friend to ask me about a crime you know I obviously was not aware of or involved in, because I'm here. I'm having a hard time trying to figure out how you've solved any crimes with this tactic."

"I got four dead detectives!" Detective Johnson snapped before banging his fist on the table. "You want to act like you don't know what I'm saying, and I'll have twenty-four-hour surveillance on your ass! You won't be able to take a shit without me knowing!"

The detective's sudden burst of anger, noise, and banging on the table made the Italian and Black

Mafia goons pull out their weapons on the detectives. Detective Wilson reacted just as fast by pulling out his 9 mm. He tried to restore order as he shifted his gun back and forth to the goons.

"Put the guns down! Detective Johnson, what the fuck is going on, man?" Detective Wilson questioned.

"Calm down, Wilson. These men aren't that stupid to kill me in broad daylight, knowing they would have to kill you too!" Johnson said as he stood from his seat. "I'll be seeing you around, Smitty. Next time I'll be coming full force!"

"Detective Johnson, you know me well, which means you know I don't do threats. Then again, we'll see how this all unfolds when and if you return."

"I will be returning, and you'll wish you chose another lifestyle!"

He tapped Wilson on the shoulder to let him know it was time to go. They got into the car and raced off angrily. He did not realize how close he was to being killed in broad daylight. None of the people around would have said a word, especially having two powerful men from two notable organizations sitting there.

Once the cops drove off, Pauly Fingers cleared his throat and sipped his lemonade before he addressed the problem Cocaine Smitty had just said he had under control.

"It's getting crazy around your neck of the woods, huh? Maybe you should think about having

Donte take care of that for you. What you think?"

"I'll have it taken care of. I don't like to be disrespected or embarrassed in front of my friends."

"Don't be embarrassed. Just handle it."

Smitty knew Pauly made the statement because it was a bad look having the detectives come to his place looking for him. This type of heat is not good at all. Donte would have to be brought in to make this all go away.

Donte was a vicious killer that loved fulfilling any contract given to him as long as the money was right and it all made sense to him. The twenty-five-year-old Italian was also the grandson of Michael Clericuzio, but he had been good friends with Cocaine Smitty for some time. He was also connected to his family roots and chased the dream

of one day being a made man himself.

Donte stood six foot even, weighed 220 pounds,

and had a medium build. He had a dark stare with

black-colored eyes and thick black eyebrows that

flowed with his silky black, combed-back hair. He

was clean-shaven and well groomed, and he looked

like a true Mafioso. Donte was the guy they sent to

track down the snitches. He would torture them for

being rats. One time he made a man's kids watch

before he killed them, too, just in case they could ID

him. Heartless, dark, cold, and calculated were the

words to best describe this Mafia assassin.

"Donte sounds like a good idea for this. I'll focus

on the loose ends so we can get back to making

money for both of our families," Cocaine Smitty said.

"Aye, call me if you need anything, all right? Don't be all stubborn like ya don't need help."

Pauly excused himself and made his way back into the deli. Smitty also left with his men in his Rolls Royce and headed back to Brooklyn to meet up with his team.

Cocaine Smitty was determined to bring an end to this beef with Young Pablo and the rest of the Spanish Harlem crew that were riding with him, especially with the loss of his number two guy and his lieutenants.

Flaco was now healed up and able to move around better than day one of being shot. He was also thinking about making his next move. He was over at the warehouse where he had been staying low watching television after seeing the breaking news about the shootout in Spanish Harlem, even showing Gordo and his sister. Right then, Flaco started feeling some guilt for their deaths since he was the one that gave up everyone's addresses, which is how they found Gordo's sister.

Cocaine Smitty walked into the warehouse, turned off the television, and stood in front of Flaco. He was mad as hell, especially after the muthafucking detective had come at him like he did.

"You started this fucking war with ya homies. Now you have to figure out some way to pay for all the men and money I've been losing! Plus, I got these muthafucking cops coming down on me about them dead detectives! More money is going to be lost."

Flaco was ready to leave and never look back or be in need of their assistance, but one thing held him up. He never got his share of the cocaine, since Blanco took it back to deceive Kitty Cat, so he was out of that deal. Now he needed money to leave the city and sustain him until he got back on his feet.

"You give me twenty-four hours and I'll come up with something that will end your beef with Young Pablo, plus get the cops off your back."

"I feel like I'm going against my better judgment, but I'll give you the time you need. But if you fall short, Young Pablo is going to be the least of your worries!"

After the little talk with Flaco, Smitty walked over to his soldiers and put them on to the game and what needed to be done next. He then headed over to the mini-bar, poured himself a drink, and looked on at the picture of Blanco and him on a yacht that had been taken last year. He raised his shot glass to the picture while looking on at his number-two guy.

"This one's for you, my nigga. We riding 'til the last breath," he said while downing the shot and then getting back to business.

He then called up Donte to secure the matters he and Pauly Fingers had talked about.

CHAPTER 15

The New York day had faded to night a few hours later, the street lights lit up, the hustlas were out getting money, and the ballas were at the clubs with the models and bottles. As for Young Pablo and his team of Cat, Mya, Princess, Chico, and Pito, they were up in another lay-low spot drinking and enjoying each other's company.

"This is for my homeboys, Gordo and Kilo. They kept it real until the end," Young Pablo toasted.

Everybody in the room looked on at Young Pablo in silence and showed their respect for the lost homies. Cat saw her baby bro grit his teeth, so she knew something, if not all of this shit, was getting to him, because he never liked to cry when they were kids either. He always wanted to be the tough one.

"Hey, brother, you good?"

"Yeah, I'm just showing the dead homies some respect. Plus, I'm thinking about getting them Black Mafia muthafuckas. Because it's not going to be over until we cut off the head of this bitch."

"We got their attention, plus we killed their number-two guy and their lieutenants," Pito reminded them. "But, they're still going to pay for what they did to Kilo, Gordo, and Gordo's sister."

"Don't lose sight of getting money. That's still our main goal, and if we're busy running around chasing after these motherfuckers, then we're not chasing paper," Princess said.

Cat smirked since she respected and understood her girl's stance, because money had been lost thus far.

Chico stood up with a bottle of tequila in hand

and poured shots for everyone before raising his glass.

"This is for power and victory. The world is all yours, Young Pablo!"

"That's the realest shit right there, Chico," Young Pablo said while raising his glass.

They drank a little more and enjoyed their time together and conversation. Young Pablo's cell phone sounded off and shifted his attention from the conversation.

"Shhh, shh! It's my peoples down in Little Havana," he said after placing his finger to his mouth indicating for everyone lower their voices. "What's up, Manuel, you good?"

"Yeah, you?"

"Making it happen one day at a time."

Manuel Colon was a Cuban-born refugee that

made his way to the States over fifteen years ago. He saw how he could make a living making money once he arrived, and he never looked back. Being broke and coming from a poor country made him appreciate every dollar he made. At the same time, it made him kill over every dollar that was owed to him. He now resided in Little Havana among the people who embraced him with love as well as feared his violent streak.

The six-foot-three 240-pound Cuban drug lord had a strong Cuban accent with an even deeper voice that was very distinguished, and he always seemed to command respect and order. He was also the person who supplied Young Pablo and fronted him three hundred kilos of grade-A cocaine, which allowed him to take over the streets of New York City with his pure product and competing prices.

"I only call for one reason, my friend. You don't usually go so long without calling me or coming to see me down here. It's been three weeks, so when will you be coming down so I can secure my money?"

The hit on Young Pablo's aunt's crib had set him back on the time factor; however, all the money he had in the streets would cover the debt he owed to Manuel. Business was going to be slow now with the cops being killed, and he knew this, but Manuel did not collect excuses. He only wanted his money.

"I got a lot going on up here, but I will have the money in a day or so. My stash house got hit, plus I'm going to war with these Black Mafia fools."

"Pablo, your problems are your problems. They don't pay me. So just get my money. You know the rules to this game: drugs, money, blood!" he said before hanging up and leaving him with those taunting words.

"Fuck you, Manuel! I'll kill these motherfuckers and then come for you!" Young Pablo snapped before he threw his phone all pissed off and drunk.

Manuel wanted his $3.45 million for the cocaine he fronted Young Pablo. It was product he could have stepped on to double his return, but he left it raw.

"Hey, Pablo, what's up, bro?"

"Manuel wants his money. He wants it now. He don't give a fuck about what's going on up here. His money is all he cares about!"

"That Cuban punta don't want war!" Catrina said in anger by the Cuban's actions that made her brother upset.

"Relax, bro. Let's enjoy our drinks and tomorrow

we'll handle the money thing with Manuel. We got it between us. We just have to stick together and think this shit out!" Chico said while drinking his beer.

They all sat back drinking and then figured out the amount they would be able to pay Manuel, because there was no need to have two wars going on at the same time.

As they figured out numbers, the Black Mafia was hitting another of their stash houses filled with money, heroin, and cocaine. It was a stash house that Young Pablo had shared with his sister, Catrina. This time slimy-ass Flaco made sure he got his cut off the top. Flaco knew that this hit on his old associates would hurt then financially, since he knew Young Pablo owed a large sum of money to the Cuban down south.

Flaco looked on at Cocaine Smitty and saw the

look of satisfaction on his face, and he knew that he bought himself some more time—certainly enough time to make his next move.

"I told you my word is good and we would all eat off this hit!" Flaco said.

Hearing Flaco speak made Cocaine Smitty realize all the chaos that had surrounded him— and because of Flaco. His smile dissipated as he became serious.

"You'll be good for now, but don't think for one second this is over, because your homeboy and his sister are going to be pissed about this loss."

"Trust me, bro. He's going to have more than you to worry about, because he owes the Cuban millions for all the cocaine he fronted him."

Smitty smirked at Flaco's every word, because he knew how the Cuban muthafuckas rolled.

"Let's take a drink to taking control of this war shit. This is to power and control!"

Everyone agreed on the toast and raised their glasses before drinking to power and control. Cocaine Smitty refilled his glass with a double shot and thought about what Flaco had just said about the Cubans. He knew if war came with them, there would not be any drive-bys. They would send a small army with fully automatic weapons. He didn't want a problem like this, so he pulled his lieutenant to the side.

"I want you to keep an eye on this muthafucka right there. I don't trust him. Also, I want to know about these Cubans down in Little Havana that Young Pablo is connected with. If they got beef, we need to know as soon as possible."

"Say no more, boss. I'm on it. My eyes and ears

are to the streets."

Cocaine Smitty turned with his glass in hand and looked back at Flaco as he gazed at the money in his hand. Smitty downed the shot while still processing his thoughts about Flaco and what he should really do because he was a traitor.

CHAPTER 16

At eight o'clock the next morning, Detective Wilson was at home preparing to head into work as he stood in the mirror adjusting his shirt that covered his bullet-proof vest. His early morning thoughts were of the downed officers. He knew he had to get closure for their families. He made his way downstairs into the kitchen to grab a glass of orange juice. After a few gulps, he holstered his weapon before making his way outside to his unmarked car.

As he made his way around to the driver's side, he noticed a face walking down the streets that was not familiar to the neighborhood. He fumbled around with his keys, since he wanted to see the guy walking down the street up close. As a detective, he was naturally curious, especially seeing a well-dressed man walking as if he had parked far away. As the man walked closer, he waved at Detective Wilson, who he realized had been watching him.

"Good morning, Detective."

"Well, so far the weather is the only good thing this morning," Detective Wilson stated sarcastically.

Wilson watched as the man continued down the street. He then got into the car and watched him through his rear-view mirror. He started the car, and at the same time a thought came to him.

"How the hell did this guy know I was a detective?"

In that very moment, Detective Wilson glanced back up at the rear-view mirror, but the man was gone—until he heard a knock on the driver's-side window. As soon as Wilson turned toward the window, he was greeted with a flash of fire. Two silenced rounds crashed into the window and entered his brain, ejecting his flesh and bones out the other side and spraying onto the passenger seat as his body slumped over.

"I guess you can say it's a bad morning for you, Detective Wilson," Donte said as he tucked away the silenced 9 mm in his waistline and walked away as if nothing had ever happened.

As he walked down the street, a 760Li BMW pulled up smoothly and then stopped alongside him. He hopped in as his driver took off from the perfect mob hit.

Donte was a perfectionist when it came to completing a job. So just like clockwork, he took Detective Wilson out knowing precisely the time he would be leaving his home.

While his driver took him to the Bronx, Donte

whipped out a valve of powder cocaine and dumped some onto his fist. He then snorted it up each nostril and immediately felt the rush of the powdery substance work its magic to his brain and through his bloodstream. It made him feel on top of the world.

"Yes! You know that's some good shit when ya face gets numb. Ya know what I'm talking about?" Donte said, feeling himself while at the same time feeling invincible. "The way I feel right now, I could wipe out the whole fucking police force, and they wouldn't even see it coming! You know what I mean? Aye, Blanco should have brought me in from the beginning with them Ricans. I would have taken them all out, even that pretty-ass sister of his. But you know everybody thinks they have the best plans. He probably was trying to keep all of the money to himself, you know, and that shit backfired on him!"

The Black Mafia associate looked on at Donte. He knew he was crazy, and the cocaine he was snorting did not help tone him down either.

"That's some good shit you're snorting, huh? It got you feeling like that, huh?" Mike asked.

Donte took another snort before addressing Mike.

"Yeah, this is it. You want some?"

"Nah, I'm good. I have to stay focused."

"What? What the fuck did you ask about it for? What is this thing about being focused? I'm focused on everything around here!"

"You look like you're feeling yourself, that's all, Donte. I didn't mean anything by it."

Donte was high and felt the rush of cocaine soar through his body and brain. At the same time, he felt the power as he pulled out his gun. He was on edge and paranoid. Mike, the Black Mafia associate, knew how Donte could be, so he remained silent the rest of the way while driving. Donte also knew that if he whacked Smitty's guy just for asking questions like that, he would have the heat brought down on him.

"You got some friggin' nerve, you know? I feel like I'm being interrogated—like you're checking up on me or something! Don't do that shit again, I tell ya, especially if you know what's good for you!" he said while looking at the driver and then back out the window. "Let's go take care of that other thing before I get off track here," he said before glancing back over at his driver.

He saw how quiet Mike had become, and he did not want to go back and forth with him. He slipped his shades on and stared out the window at the streets of New York City. He was still feeling the power of the cocaine and the gun he had in his grip. He wanted to make a statement on this next job he had to take care of, so others knew not to ever disrespect the Black Mafia.

CHAPTER 17

At 9:45 a.m. Detective Johnson pulled up to his partner's house after being made aware of the slaying. He wanted to see for himself what had happened to give him an idea of how everything unfolded. He had an idea of who was responsible and had the balls to pull off something like this. As soon as he exited his car, he was greeted by the first officer to respond to the call.

"Detective Johnson, I'm Officer Andrews, first on the scene. My take on this is a robbery gone bad or a random act of violence. You know with all these up-and-coming gangs and their initiation rituals?"

"Are you kidding me, Andrews? Do you see how my partner was killed? Does this look random to you? This is a Mafia gang-land-style killing.

Detective Wilson was always alert of his surroundings. He would have never let anyone just walk up on him like this, so we're dealing with a professional hit man that would move swiftly yet unnoticed," he explained before pausing and then looking at his partner's lifeless body slumped over in the seat. It then came to him. "Officer Andrews, please hit up my phone if something changes. I'll let the homicide crew over here handle this one."

He then ran back to his car. When he got back to his car, he put his head on the steering wheel and thought about seeing his lifeless partner.

"You muthafucking bastards! Why him?" he yelled out, pounding on the steering wheel.

Detective Johnson realized that whoever was responsible might never see a courtroom if he got to them first. He composed himself long enough to drive off and head to the Bronx in search of Cocaine Smitty.

As Detective Johnson drove to the Bronx, he could not get the image of his lifeless partner out of his mind. He wanted to find out who put the hit out on him. More importantly, in his anger and emotional rage, who would be the one to receive his wrath that would be coming their way?

CHAPTER 18

Within minutes, Detective Johnson was flying down the street with his sirens blaring and lights flashing. He put his foot to the gas until he arrived in front of the deli. His abrupt stop made his tires screech. Pauly Fingers was inside the deli and thought that a young punk had driven by and made all the noise. Detective Johnson rushed into the deli and yelled out, which disturbed the customers inside and offended Pauly Fingers.

"Where's that piece of shit friend of yours? I know he had my partner whacked this morning. You must have known this was going to take place too."

Pauly felt disrespected by these outrageous allegations. Normally he would have his guys snatch him up and take him to the back to deal with him, but in this very moment, he had to have some control because of the customers inside his deli. Besides, he did not need any more police trouble around. Pauly's guys ran over behind the detective and apologized for not stopping him from running inside like that.

"Sorry, Pauly, we didn't know he was going to come up in here like that."

"No need to apologize. The detective here is the one that should be saying he's sorry for coming in here and making noise and false accusations, as if he freaking lost his mind or something. You should calm down and talk like you have some professional sense," Pauly said, trying to remain calm yet commanding.

"I'll calm down all right. If I find out you're protecting that son of a bitch, you'll fall just as hard as he will! You don't go around whacking cops like you're in the old days and get away with it!"

"What, is this friggin' guy crazy? Are you threatening me? Get him outta here already. He's distracting my customers," Pauly demanded.

Pauly was so pissed off that he was ready to put a bullet into the head of Detective Johnson.

"Get the fuck off of me! I came in here by myself, and I'll leave without your hands all over me!" Detective Johnson snapped, not wanting the Mafia goons touching him.

Once he left, Pauly made his way around the deli and apologized to his customers.

"Sorry, folks. This maniac came in here like he was on drugs or something. Anyway, all your meals are on me today."

Once he made good with his customers, he made a call to Cocaine Smitty, who picked up immediately when he saw the incoming call.

"Aye, your crazy cop just came over here acting like a friggin' fool. Is this guy on speed or something? He came in here like he don't know what's good for him! I thought you had this thing under control and taken care of."

"I put that in motion already. I don't know what the hold-up is. It's never like this, you know."

"Well, be on the lookout because this guy is running wild, and it's not good for business, you know?"

"I understand. I got it, Pauly. I'll check on the progress of this situation after we hang up."

After the call, Pauly's crew came over to him. They knew he needed to speak with them about what had just taken place.

"What do ya wanna do about the mall cop,

Pauly?"

"He's going to be dealt with. I do have something else I need to take care of, but right now I have to go pay my financial respects to Don Clericuzio. Then we'll discuss that other thing later."

As Pauly made his way to his Lincoln Town Car, where his driver awaited, he saw the 760Li BMW pull up, roll down the window, and expose Donte's face.

"Aye, I thought you were supposed to take care of this thing over there? Are you slacking on me?"

"This friggin' guy wasn't there, so what do you want me to do?"

"I want you to take care of it. He just came past here like a tornado. I can't have guys like this coming around. It's not good for business, plus I could have had the don here, and you know how that would have turned out?"

"I got this, Uncle Pauly, trust me. Have I ever let you down?" Donte responded before he paused to snort a line of cocaine off his fist.

Pauly saw this and became upset, since he was unaware that his nephew did this type of thing that was forbidden by the don and rest of family.

"Aye, leave that shit alone already!"

"Don't worry, Uncle Pauly. I'm in control of this over here."

"You better be in control. There's no room for mistakes or that shit you're putting up your nose!"

Donte smirked as he hit the switch and rolled up the dark-tinted windows. His driver took off and headed toward the next stop to take out the detective. Pauly got into his car and had his driver take him to the don's mansion on Long Island.

CHAPTER 19

Pauly arrived at the don's house and had his driver pull into the circular driveway. He immediately took notice of all of the cars there. It was not a holiday, so he questioned why there were so many cars.

"What do you make of all these cars here? It looks like the heads of the families or something," Pauly said to his driver.

"I don't know, Pauly. Maybe something came up and they needed to deal with it?"

"I guess I'm about to find out. I'll be in and out. I'ma drop the money off and pay my financial respects."

"I'll keep the car running."

Pauly took the bag of money containing

$300,000 in cash, which was the Don's cut from all of his secret businesses and shake-downs from the unions and construction. As soon as he entered the house, he was greeted with love by other Mafia associates.

"Pauly Fingers, how the hell are ya doing over there in the Bronx?"

"I'm moving around, so I can't complain, Joey. How are things down in Miami with you and your crew? I see you got that million-dollar look going on with the golden tan and all."

"I'm doing good down there. You have to come visit and get some of the sun and good life down there."

"Yeah, I'll come down soon. Make sure ya have

some of them Miami babes for me."

Joey "Outlaw" Catillino was a Mafia capo for the Clericuzio family down in Florida, where he kept the casinos and other family interests in line. Joey earned his nickname from the way he was banned from the casinos in Las Vegas. The sixty-five-year-old looked more like fifty-five, especially since he had worked out so much in his younger days, which preserved him until he stopped. Nowadays, he was living the good life. He still would chop a body up if he had to, just like he did in the old days. In fact, he once chopped up a capo from another family and fed his body down the garbage disposal. It was a real mess, but he was that pissed.

"Aye, Joey what's with all the cars out front?"

"I don't really know, Pauly. I just came to pay my financial respect. I did see the four other dons here, so it could be anything, you know?"

Pauly mingled and spoke with a few other made men before the don came downstairs to make his presence felt as the goombahs in the room all shifted their attention. They all smiled and nodded their heads to acknowledge his presence.

The silver-haired don had grayish eyes that could see through any bullshit. At eighty years of age, he had seen his fair share of life and all that it had entailed, especially in La Cosa Nostra. Don Clericuzio favored the late Don Carlo Gambino, who was a real gangster and mobster.

"Pauly Fingers, you look great. How's business

treating you?" Don Clericuzio asked.

"I'm making it happen over there, ya know?"

Pauly knew he only looked good to the don because he was holding a bag of money that he knew was for him. He opened the bag and displayed the cash. The don took the bag as he continued speaking.

"I guess things are going great for you in the Bronx?"

"Like I said, I'm trying to make it happen. Anything for you and this family."

The don took a step closer and leaned in to speak in a lower tone, so he could be discreet. "What do you know about that thing that's been all over the news this morning?"

Pauly knew what the don was referring to. In fact,

a part of him wanted to act as if he did not know what the don was talking about, but it was too close to his deli and where he ran his business in the streets.

"You talking about that pig?"

"Yeah, this guy was making moves for the Genovese Family, which is why the heads are here to figure out who was responsible for this thing since he was in for $5 million. He was moving their money around or something of that nature. The thing is, only he knew where the money was, so you know that things like this just don't go away. Somebody will have to pay, ya know?"

Pauly's mind raced while thinking about his involvement. He was not trying to take the fall for it nor pay the $5 million, so he stuck to his original line and lie.

"I don't know nothing about that or who did it, but I will have my guys put their ears to the streets. Anything for the family."

Don Clericuzio patted Pauly on the shoulder. He then looked him in the eyes and felt like he had just been lied to, which would not be good for Pauly.

"Take care of yourself, Pauly. I'll see ya later. Maybe I'll stop by your place for lunch soon."

"I'll have something from the old country waiting for you."

"The best meats, fresh bread, and olive oil. Bellisimo!" he said, flashing back to his time in Italy as a child.

Pauly exited the mansion, got into his car, and

immediately called up Donte to inform him of the conversation he had with the don, because it was clean-up time and the other pig needed to go now. The phone just rang, which pissed Pauly off even more.

"Pick up the friggin' phone, ya schmuck!"

The driver took Pauly back to the deli as he continued trying to dial up Donte. He did not want this shit to get out of hand. Donte finally answered his phone.

"Uncle Pauly, what's going on now?"

"I hope ya taking care of that other thing now, because that first thing is causing big problems at the old man's place. The first guy I just found out was into another family for $5 million, and you know that a thing like that isn't going to just go away!"

"Ya busting my balls over here. I'm moving as fast as I can without slipping or getting caught."

"I'm just busting ya balls! But you know what could happen if this thing goes wrong. You won't have any balls to bust!"

"All right already, I'm here and ready to make sure this problem goes away, and then I'll be over to your place, okay?" he said before hanging up and feeling the pressure coming down on him.

CHAPTER 20

Donte sat out in front of the police station waiting down the street and watching Detective Johnson's car. The good detective was inside filling out his daily log before going out into the field. Donte sat there thinking about what his uncle just had said to him. This was not good, so now he had to take care of this and hope this pig did not owe anyone.

"Aye, Mike, you know that pig I put down earlier was into another family for $5 million? Who would have ever thought that could be? Ya never know who's crooked these days!" Donte said.

"All of them pigs can be turned for the right price," Mike began. "That's ya boy right there coming out."

Detective Johnson walked out looking around to

make sure no one came up on him fast with a gun out.

"Yeah, that's him. Let's go, ya piece of shit! People are getting their balls busted around here because of you."

Johnson even looked under his car and checked for explosives, because he felt the bullets his partner took were meant for him. He did not realize that he was responsible for sealing both of their fates.

Before Detective Johnson could look under his car and see the explosives mounted beneath the driver's side, Donte approached out of the blue. He spoke just as quickly and tried to distract Johnson from looking under that side of the car.

"Detective Johnson, sir! Detective Johnson!"

Donte was casually dressed and looked the part of a young businessman on Wall Street. Detective

Johnson was still paranoid, so he made sure he was on point and alert. As the man approached him fast, he kept his hand on his sidearm while looking over at the man calling out to him.

Donte did not want to detonate the explosives while the detective was standing on the outside of the car, because if he survived, it would not be good.

"Detective Johnson, I know this may sound crazy, but a co-worker of mine told me she saw who killed that detective this morning. I told her to come down to the station, but she's nervous and afraid of being seen."

"This better not be some bullshit! What's this friend's name?"

"Deborah Estill. She lives directly across from the detective."

"This better he a good lead or I'll come find you.

I remember faces."

Detective Johnson got into his car and raced off. At the same time Donte's driver pulled up and picked him up. As the detective turned the corner, instinct made him look into his rear-view mirror. Donte looked back at him with a sadistic grin. At that same moment, he pressed the button and detonated the explosives that ripped through the car and instantly killed the detective, engulfing his flesh and bones in flames. The ground around shook and set off car alarms and shattered glass windows, alerting all around.

Donte had his driver take him back to the Bronx over to Pauly's place.

Meanwhile, down in Florida in Little Havana, Manuel was becoming impatient with Young Pablo's delay and slow progress in bringing him his money.

Manuel and his associates were sitting around the table outside his Cuban restaurant playing dominos, drinking beer, and smoking fine cigars that he had smuggled in.

"Hey, José, what's up with my friend in New York? You think he's trying to play me for my money?"

"He's never late with the money. When people do things like this, it means he's either in jail or he thinks he can take you for your money, boss."

Manuel did not like what he was hearing or thinking, and this showed as he slammed down the dominos harder than usual. The Cuban drug lord was pissed. The only thing that could make him feel better was his money or Young Pablo's blood. Nothing else mattered at this point.

"I tried calling him three times today, and he does

not answer. I think it's time someone went to get his attention."

Manuel did not know that Young Pablo's phone was broken. He could only call out, and he did not notice that he could not receive calls. This was neither good nor a good look for him.

"I'll take care of this for you, boss. It'll be fun," José responded with a smirk.

"I don't want fun! I want my fucking money!"

"I got this, Manuel. He won't even see it coming!"

"His life means nothing to me if he can't pay. Get the money and leave him there."

CHAPTER 21

A few days had passed by, and the New York City
Police Department was enraged by the murders of
Detectives Johnson and Wilson, along with the
others massacred at Young Pablo's lay-low spot. The
fact that they did not have any leads on these murders
angered them even more. Multiple arrests had been
made in an attempt to get resolve, but to no avail,
because most of these guys had lawyered up leading
to their release.

The police pressure was making it harder for the
Black Mafia and Young Pablo's team to get money.

Young Pablo, Chico, and Pito were over at a
bodega in Spanish Harlem counting up what money
they did make to send back down to Little Havana.
Young Pablo really wanted to pay off Manuel now

so he could keep the flow going and bounce back from the loss he had taken with Flaco giving up both of his stash houses.

While they were in the back of the bodega getting the money together, the front of the store was being run by a Spanish mami that Young Pablo fucked with on the side.

Kitty Cat and her girls were over at her high-rise counting up what she had to give to her baby brother to make it right with Manuel. They figured that keeping the flow with him would allow both of them to get back to where they were before this war shit. After she got the money together, she called up her baby bro. His phone rang over and over with no answer, which worried her. She hung up and then called Pito, since she knew they were together. He saw that Cat was calling, so he picked right up.

"Hey, what's up, mami?"

"Pito, where is my brother?"

"Here, mami. Just a minute. Hey, Pablo, it's your sister."

He then tossed the phone over to Young Pablo, who wondered why she had not called his phone.

"Hey, sis."

"What's up with your phone? I called that shit a few times and it's just ringing."

"I got my phone right here in front of me. It works because I called Pito and Chico earlier."

"It must not be receiving calls. Just get a new one, because you can't afford to miss money calls. Anyway, what are you doing over there?"

"Trying to get this paper together. How you looking over there?"

"I got half a mil for you. We can get the rest from

the Black Mafia once we hit them for what they stole from your spot."

Before he could respond, he saw that his little mami up in the front of the store had pressed the button that made a light in the back flash red, which was used to get his attention. He then looked at the monitor and saw a couple standing in front of the cash register.

"Hey, Chico. Go see what they want and who they are, bro."

"Alright, I got this," he said, standing up and looking at the monitor. "Damn, mami got a fat ass, too," he said while walking through the door to the front of the store.

Young Pablo focused back on his count and talking to his sister on the phone. As Chico walked through the door, he saw a couple that he had never seen before. They did not look like cops unless they were deep undercover.

"What's going on? Who are you and what do you want?"

"Our names are not that important. Where's your boss?" the silky black-haired Cuban with greenish eyes immediately replied, which alarmed Chico.

Her questioning gave Chico a bad vibe about these two. They were definitely not cops. Chico put his hand on the gun in his waistline for them to see clearly, because their body language did not match their smiles.

"My boss is busy right now, plus he doesn't meet people without names or reasons to see him."

The Cuban male did not even give his female friend a chance to say anything else, because he was there to take care of business. He pulled out his nickel-plated long-barrel .44 Magnum at the same time and pulled back the hammer with his thumb. He was obviously making a power statement. "Don't even think about grabbing that gun, or I'll blow your fucking brains out, asshole!"

Chico was a true gangsta, and he wanted to show his loyalty for Young Pablo. He did not want these muthafuckas to get the drop on his homie, because he knew they were from Little Havana, so he yelled out, "Pablo! It's a hit!"

Pito and Young Pablo turned toward the monitor and saw Chico reach for his gun, so they grabbed their heat too.

Chico got off a round and hit the female, which thrust her body into the shelf of chips. Chico also got caught at point-blank range and was hit with the massive slugs from the .44 Magnum.

Cat was still on the phone with her baby brother when she heard the commotion.

"Cat, that punta Manuel put a hit out on me. They're here now!"

When Cat heard this, her heart sunk when she thought of the worst. At the same time, she reacted just as quickly and rounded up her girls to ride out.

"We have to go! They're trying to kill my brother," Cat yelled as she rushed out of the high-rise.

Once the Cuban gunned down Chico where he stood, he made his way back toward the door that led to the back office. His lady friend recovered from the slug that slammed into her small frame. Although she was hurt, she knew that she, too, came to do a job. The two Cubans came through the back door and were greeted with multiple slugs fired at them.

"Die, bitch!" Pito yelled out in between bursts of gunfire.

He saw that he had hit the female with his barrage of slugs, as her frame thrust back into the store front.

The other Cuban took cover as the bullets tore through the door and frame, which sent shrapnel everywhere.

"You stupid asshole! You know you're going to die! Manuel doesn't play about his money, muthafucka!"

"Fuck you! Fuck Manuel! I got the money, you stupid muthafucka, but you won't see a dime of that shit now!"

"You won't live long enough to spend Manuel's money, fool!"

The Cuban fired off a round into the back room and missed, but it crashed into the wall behind Young

Pablo.

Pito knew he could hold off the Cuban while his homeboy slipped out the back door, so he brought it to his attention.

"Hey, grab the money and hit the back door. I got this muthafucka right here. He'll die trying to come up in here!"

Young Pablo started stuffing the bags of money but kept his eye on the door where the Cuban was standing on the other side. He was trying to come through the back to get at him.

"Hey, Pito! Meet me over at Cat's spot as soon as you're outta this muthafucka!"

"You already know he ain't going nowhere except to the graveyard. I'ma lay his bitch ass down!"

Young Pablo threw the duffle bag over his

shoulder and then tucked his gun in his waistline as he headed toward the back door to slip out. As soon as he opened the door, to his surprise, he came face-to-face with a .45 Desert Eagle staring back at him. On the other side of the gun was Manuel's number two guy and enforcer, José.

"Where are you going, my friend? Nobody fucks with Manuel's money!"

Before Young Pablo could say a word or react and grab his gun from his waistline, José pulled the trigger twice, which sent unforgiving slugs into Young Pablo's face. His head snapped back with brute force, breaking his neck while at the same time ejecting his brains and skull bones out the other side. He was dead before his body even hit the ground. The life of New York's youngest kingpin was no more.

Pito immediately shifted his attention and weapon toward the sound and sight of his fallen homie. He opened fire toward the back door shooting in José's direction, but he forgot about the first Cuban. He was reminded of his presence when the thug fired off slugs from his powerful .44 Magnum that slammed into Pito's body, which instantly dropped him as his body twisted from the power of the bullets crashing into him.

José calmly walked over to the downed young thug and saw that he was barely breathing with wounds to his lung and internal organs.

"Your team was never built for this war shit. You don't have enough money or power," José said smoothly, being in power.

"Fuck! Fuck you! I can kill all of you Cubans by myself!" Pito shouted, still wanting to be a fighter until the end.

"Maybe in another lifetime, but not this one," José said before pumping a few rounds into his chest that made his body flop off the ground as each slug pounded into his flesh and sucked the life from him.

José turned around and saw the money on the table as well as the bag that Young Pablo seemed to grip even in death.

"Mira, get the money over there, plus the bag he's holding onto."

Once they secured the money, they headed back down to Little Havana to relay the good news to Manuel.

CHAPTER 22

Within minutes Cat, Princess, and Mya showed up at the bodega, just after the police had arrived and started to secure the scene. They parked their bikes and rushed over to the bodega. They wanted to know what was going on, because Cat's instincts and the sight of yellow tape meant there were bodies inside. Cat bypassed the cops and rushed into the back of the bodega, only to see her baby brother lying lifeless in a puddle of his own blood. The cops rushed in behind Cat to see what was going on with her and why she had slipped passed them like that.

"Oh my God! No! No! No! Not my brother!" Cat yelled out, crying when she saw her brother's lifeless flesh.

She dropped to her knees as if the sight of her

brother halted her power and will to walk. Mya and Princess were at her side and were just as emotional upon seeing him massacred like this. Her pain burned deep to her core, but at the same time, she wanted nothing more than revenge for this.

"Whatever you want to do, ma, we down. The have to pay for this by any means!" Princess said as she wiped away her tears and was ready to draw blood from those that did this.

"We'll get them fools for my beloved brother!" Cat cried while standing to her feet, before kissing her hand and blowing it toward her baby brother's lifeless body. "I won't let them get away, baby bro. On my life, I promise," she said before she turned to walk out with her girls ready to get revenge now.

"We should fly down to Little Havana tonight and catch them off guard. They don't know us nor will they be expecting to be taken out by three bad bitches like us," Mya said while wiping her eyes and sniffling.

"I want their blood for this. I want him to suffer just as my brother did. I know he'll be protected with his goons around him, so we have to come with our best game to get these fools. But keep in mind, this is Florida. We have to look the part and play them puntas until we shed their blood," Catrina said, trying to pull herself together while at the same time ready to deal with these motherfuckers that brought this pain into her heart.

Flaco would also get his for starting all this off, but for now, Manuel was her target.

"I'm going to ride or die with you, mami," Princess said.

"Me too, Cat. We've been homegirls for a while,

and you've showed me nothing but love!" Mya added.

They all came together and gave each other a hug before focusing back on heading down to Little Havana. They got themselves together along with the money they would need to look the part. They then chanted to fit in before catching the first flight out.

To order books, please fill out the order form below:
To order films please go to www.good2gofilms.com

Name: _____

Address: _____

City: _____ State: _____ Zip Code: _____

Phone: _____

Email: _____

Method of Payment: Check   VISA   MASTERCARD

Credit Card#: _____

Name as it appears on card: _____

Signature: _____

Item Name	Price	Qty	Amount
48 Hours to Die – Silk White	$14.99		
A Hustler's Dream - Ernest Morris	$14.99		
A Hustler's Dream 2 - Ernest Morris	$14.99		
A Thug's Devotion – J. L. Rose and J. M. McMillon	$14.99		
All Eyes on Tommy Gunz – Warren Holloway	$14.99		
Black Reign – Ernest Morris	$14.99		
Bloody Mayhem Down South – Trayvon Jackson	$14.99		
Bloody Mayhem Down South 2 – Trayvon Jackson	$14.99		
Business Is Business – Silk White	$14.99		
Business Is Business 2 – Silk White	$14.99		
Business Is Business 3 – Silk White	$14.99		
Cash In Cash Out – Assa Raymond Baker	$14.99		
Cash In Cash Out 2 - Assa Raymond Baker	$14.99		
Childhood Sweethearts – Jacob Spears	$14.99		
Childhood Sweethearts 2 – Jacob Spears	$14.99		
Childhood Sweethearts 3 - Jacob Spears	$14.99		
Childhood Sweethearts 4 - Jacob Spears	$14.99		
Connected To The Plug – Dwan Marquis Williams	$14.99		
Connected To The Plug 2 – Dwan Marquis Williams	$14.99		
Connected To The Plug 3 – Dwan Williams	$14.99		
Cost of Betrayal – W.C. Holloway	$14.99		
Cost of Betrayal 2 – W.C. Holloway	$14.99		
Deadly Reunion – Ernest Morris	$14.99		
Dream's Life – Assa Raymond Baker	$14.99		
Flipping Numbers – Ernest Morris	$14.99		

Flipping Numbers 2 – Ernest Morris	$14.99		
He Loves Me, He Loves You Not - Mychea	$14.99		
He Loves Me, He Loves You Not 2 - Mychea	$14.99		
He Loves Me, He Loves You Not 3 - Mychea	$14.99		
He Loves Me, He Loves You Not 4 – Mychea	$14.99		
He Loves Me, He Loves You Not 5 – Mychea	$14.99		
Killing Signs – Ernest Morris	$14.99		
Kings of the Block – Dwan Willams	$14.99		
Kings of the Block 2 – Dwan Willams	$14.99		
Lord of My Land – Jay Morrison	$14.99		
Lost and Turned Out – Ernest Morris	$14.99		
Love & Dedication – W.C. Holloway	$14.99		
Love Hates Violence – De'Wayne Maris	$14.99		
Love Hates Violence 2 – De'Wayne Maris	$14.99		
Love Hates Violence 3 – De'Wayne Maris	$14.99		
Love Hates Violence 4 – De'Wayne Maris	$14.99		
Married To Da Streets – Silk White	$14.99		
M.E.R.C. - Make Every Rep Count Health and Fitness	$14.99		
Mercenary In Love – J.L. Rose & J.L. Turner	$14.99		
Money Make Me Cum – Ernest Morris	$14.99		
My Besties – Asia Hill	$14.99		
My Besties 2 – Asia Hill	$14.99		
My Besties 3 – Asia Hill	$14.99		
My Besties 4 – Asia Hill	$14.99		
My Boyfriend's Wife - Mychea	$14.99		
My Boyfriend's Wife 2 – Mychea	$14.99		
My Brothers Envy – J. L. Rose	$14.99		
My Brothers Envy 2 – J. L. Rose	$14.99		
Naughty Housewives – Ernest Morris	$14.99		
Naughty Housewives 2 – Ernest Morris	$14.99		
Naughty Housewives 3 – Ernest Morris	$14.99		
Naughty Housewives 4 – Ernest Morris	$14.99		
Never Be The Same – Silk White	$14.99		
Shades of Revenge – Assa Raymond Baker	$14.99		

Slumped – Jason Brent	$14.99		
Someone's Gonna Get It – Mychea	$14.99		
Stranded – Silk White	$14.99		
Supreme & Justice – Ernest Morris	$14.99		
Supreme & Justice 2 – Ernest Morris	$14.99		
Supreme & Justice 3 – Ernest Morris	$14.99		
Tears of a Hustler - Silk White	$14.99		
Tears of a Hustler 2 - Silk White	$14.99		
Tears of a Hustler 3 - Silk White	$14.99		
Tears of a Hustler 4- Silk White	$14.99		
Tears of a Hustler 5 – Silk White	$14.99		
Tears of a Hustler 6 – Silk White	$14.99		
The Last Love Letter – Warren Holloway	$14.99		
The Last Love Letter 2 – Warren Holloway	$14.99		
The Panty Ripper - Reality Way	$14.99		
The Panty Ripper 3 – Reality Way	$14.99		
The Solution – Jay Morrison	$14.99		
The Teflon Queen – Silk White	$14.99		
The Teflon Queen 2 – Silk White	$14.99		
The Teflon Queen 3 – Silk White	$14.99		
The Teflon Queen 4 – Silk White	$14.99		
The Teflon Queen 5 – Silk White	$14.99		
The Teflon Queen 6 - Silk White	$14.99		
The Vacation – Silk White	$14.99		
Tied To A Boss - J.L. Rose	$14.99		
Tied To A Boss 2 - J.L. Rose	$14.99		
Tied To A Boss 3 - J.L. Rose	$14.99		
Tied To A Boss 4 - J.L. Rose	$14.99		
Tied To A Boss 5 - J.L. Rose	$14.99		
Time Is Money - Silk White	$14.99		
Tomorrow's Not Promised – Robert Torres	$14.99		
Tomorrow's Not Promised 2 – Robert Torres	$14.99		
Two Mask One Heart – Jacob Spears and Trayvon Jackson	$14.99		
Two Mask One Heart 2 – Jacob Spears and Trayvon Jackson	$14.99		

Two Mask One Heart 3 – Jacob Spears and Trayvon Jackson	$14.99		
Wrong Place Wrong Time – Silk White	$14.99		
Young Goonz – Reality Way	$14.99		
Subtotal:			
Tax:			
Shipping (Free) U.S. Media Mail:			
Total:			

Make Checks Payable To: Good2Go Publishing, 7311 W Glass Lane, Laveen, AZ 85339